Burning For Her

VA Browning

Nickanny Publishing

Contents

Smoke and Steel

♥

"**A**gain!" I roared, my voice echoing off the concrete walls of the Copper Ridge Fire Station bay.

My crew moved. Javi Martinez had the hose coupling locked in under three seconds. Luke Thompson fumbled, his young hands shaking with the effort, but he got there. They were good. They'd be better.

The morning air was thick with diesel fumes and the metallic tang of yesterday's smoke still clinging to the engines. Sunlight slanted through the open bay doors, cutting sharp angles across the polished concrete floor. This place—every inch of it—was mine. My responsibility. My crew. My family.

I'd built this team from nothing after the last chief retired and the town council nearly shuttered the whole operation. Fought for every piece of equipment, every certification, every dollar.

"Bring it in," I called, clapping my hands once. The sound cracked through the bay like a gunshot. "Good work. Thompson, ten more reps on those couplings before breakfast."

"Yes, Chief!" Luke's face was flushed, eager.

Javi wiped his forehead with his sleeve as he approached, a knowing grin tugging at the corner of his mouth. "You're gonna scare him back to his daddy's dealership."

"Better scared than dead." I grabbed a towel, swiped it across the back of my neck. "He hesitates like that in a real fire, someone doesn't come home."

"Speaking of things that don't come home..." Javi's grin faded. "State inspector's due at ten hundred."

My face went hard. "Don't remind me."

"Just saying, Jefe. Might want to put on a clean shirt. Maybe smile."

"I'll smile when they send someone who's actually fought a fire instead of just read about them." I threw the towel onto the bench harder than necessary. Inspections were a waste of time. Some desk jockey from Denver with a clipboard and a rulebook, here to justify their paycheck by finding problems that didn't exist.

The purr of an engine cut through my thoughts—too smooth, too expensive. A black SUV rolled into the lot, so pristine it looked like it had just driven off a showroom floor. Everything about it screamed money and city.

The driver's door opened.

A high heel—red-soled, probably cost more than my truck payment—touched the asphalt. Then a leg. Long, lean, encased in charcoal gray that fit like it had been tailored specifically for her body. The woman who emerged moved with the kind of precision that came from absolute control. Black hair pulled into a bun so tight it had to hurt. Sunglasses that hid half her face but somehow made her more intimidating.

She pulled the sunglasses off, and I forgot how to breathe.

Dark eyes—almost black—swept over my station with the clinical assessment of a surgeon looking for something to cut. High cheekbones. Full lips pressed into a serious line. Porcelain skin that had probably never seen a real day's work.

She was beautiful. Infuriatingly, devastatingly beautiful.

And everything about her was wrong for this place.

Her heels clicked against the concrete as she approached—sharp, rhythmic, like a countdown. I was still in a sweat-soaked t-shirt and turnout pants. I smelled like smoke and diesel. Good. Maybe it would send her running back to whatever climate-controlled office she'd crawled out of.

"Chief Drake?" Her voice was cool, professional. No warmth. No pleasantries.

"That's me." I crossed my arms over my chest.

"Inspector Lily Zhang, State Fire Marshal's Office." She held up an ID badge. Didn't offer her hand. Her gaze had already moved past me, cataloging, judging. Hairs rose on the back of my neck.

"Welcome to Copper Ridge," I said.

She didn't acknowledge the greeting. Her attention had locked onto the equipment racks. "Your SCBA bottles. When was the last hydrostatic test?"

I blinked. We hadn't even made it inside. "Due next month. Supply chain delays."

"State regulation 8 CCR 1507-1 doesn't have a provision for supply chain delays, Chief Drake." She produced a tablet from her leather bag, made a note with quick, efficient strokes. "Equipment is either compliant or it isn't."

She moved past me toward the engine bay, and floral perfume cut through diesel and smoke. I followed, my crew watching with wide eyes.

"I'll need your maintenance logs, training certifications, and the incident report from the structure fire on March fifteenth," she said, not looking at me.

"We'll get you whatever you need."

She stopped at the turnout gear racks, ran a finger along one of the coats. "This gear is over ten years old."

"It's maintained. Inspected quarterly. It keeps my crew safe."

"It's a carcinogen risk and a direct violation of NFPA 1851." She made another note. "Automatic deficiency."

Fire spread up my neck. "It's also what the town budget allows for. We work with what we have, Inspector. This isn't Denver."

"The fire doesn't care about your budget, Chief." Her eyes met mine, and for the first time something beneath the ice shone in them. Steel. Conviction. This wasn't just a job to her. She believed this. "Neither do the widows."

The words struck bone-deep, but I didn't back down. "My crew trains harder than any department in the state. We know this equipment inside and out. We know our town, our risks, our people. That's worth more than a newer model that some committee decided was five percent safer."

"Statistics would disagree with you."

"Statistics don't run into burning buildings."

Her lips thinned. For a second, something flickered in her eyes—pain, maybe, or memory—but it was gone before I could read it. "Your station response time to the Patterson warehouse fire was forty-seven seconds slower than NFPA standards."

"We had to wait for mutual aid. We're a crew of five, and that fire needed twelve."

"Which brings us to staffing levels." Another note on her tablet. "Insufficient for a town of this size."

"Insufficient for a town with money, maybe." I stepped closer, and she held her ground. I had eight inches on her, but she didn't flinch. "You want to tell me where I'm supposed to find three more qualified firefighters willing to work for thirty-eight thousand a year? You want to tell the town council they need to double our budget? Be my guest, Inspector. I've been trying for five years."

"I'm not here to solve your budgetary problems. I'm here to determine if this station meets minimum safety standards." Her voice was crisp, clinical. "So far, it doesn't."

We stood there, two feet apart, the air between us crackling with a tension I didn't want to examine too closely. Her eyes were harder than stone, but her pulse fluttered at the base of her throat. She wasn't as unaffected as she pretended.

Neither was I. And that pissed me off more than anything she'd said.

"I've seen enough for my preliminary assessment," she said finally, stepping back. Breaking whatever current had been running between us. She tapped something on her tablet.

Relief flooded through me. She'd write us up, we'd pay the fine, and she'd leave.

Then she looked up, and I saw the executioner's blade in her eyes.

"I'll need to be embedded here for the full audit," she said. "My preliminary findings indicate a two-week observation period will be necessary to determine if this station can be brought into compliance or if it needs to be decommissioned."

Two weeks.

The words sucked all the air out of the bay.

Decommissioned. She was talking about shutting us down. Shutting down the only thing standing between Copper Ridge and disaster. The thing I'd bled for. The crew I'd built.

Two weeks of this impossible, infuriating woman in my station, watching my every move, waiting for me to fail.

My jaw went rigid, so hard I felt my teeth grind. "When do you start?"

"I already have." She slid the tablet back into her bag. "I'll need an office space and access to all your files."

She turned on her expensive heel and walked back toward her pristine SUV, leaving me standing in the bay with my crew and the wreckage of my morning.

Javi let out a low whistle. "Well, Jefe. That went great."

I watched her drive away, my hands curled into fists.

Two weeks. Two weeks of fighting for my station's survival. Two weeks of trying not to notice the way her lips curved when she was about to deliver a killing blow, or the way her eyes flashed when I pushed back.

Two weeks to figure out which was going to break first—my station or my self-control.

I was betting on the station.

The Inspector's Wall

♥

T he desk was smaller than I'd expected—shoved into the corner of Mason Drake's office like an afterthought. Wyatt's desk, the crew had mentioned. The younger brother who only came to town a few times a year.

Now it was mine. For two weeks, anyway.

I set my laptop down with precise care, aligned parallel to the desk edge. Backup charger on the left. Phone on the right. Color-coded file folders—red for violations, yellow for compliance issues, green for approved systems—stacked by priority. Emergency kit in the bottom drawer: granola bars, ibuprofen, antacids.

These small rituals kept the chaos at bay.

I sat, spine straight, shoulders back. Forty-three station inspections in the last eighteen months. This was just number forty-four.

Except I couldn't stop my gaze from drifting to the window.

The training yard stretched behind the station—packed dirt, equipment obstacles, a drill tower. And Mason Drake, shirtless in the afternoon sun, putting his crew through their paces.

Focus on the compliance documentation. Focus on anything else.

I didn't look away.

He moved like controlled violence—all deliberate power and precise motion. Muscles shifted under sun-darkened skin as he demonstrated a hose carry technique. The crew watched with the kind of attention that couldn't be faked. Respect earned, not demanded.

The younger one—Thompson—mirrored the movement. Another firefighter tried, stumbled, reset. Mason's hand came down on the man's shoulder. Correcting. Teaching.

A good leader, then.

It didn't change anything. Good leaders got people killed when they cut corners. When they relied on gut instead of protocol. When they thought experience trumped regulations written in blood.

Derek had been a good leader too.

My throat tightened. I forced my attention back to the screen.

Do your job, Lily.

Inspector Zhang - Preliminary findings due Friday. Final determination required within 14 days of initial inspection per State Code 8-CCR-1507-3. Station must demonstrate compliance trajectory or face immediate operational review.

Friday. Five days away. I'd catalogued seventeen violations, any three of which could justify closure.

The door banged open.

I jerked upright, pulse spiking, hand flying to my heart.

Mason filled the doorway, still shirtless, a towel slung around his neck. Sweat gleamed on his shoulders. He smelled like exertion and smoke and pine—clean and masculine and entirely too distracting.

"Need the personnel files." He moved past me toward the filing cabinet like I was furniture.

I swiveled to face him, grateful my voice came out level. "You could knock."

"It's my office." He yanked open a drawer, rifled through folders. A pale scar ran along his left forearm. Old burn, probably.

Stop looking at his arms.

"Shared office," I said. "For the next two weeks."

"Don't remind me." He found his file, slammed the drawer.

Silence stretched. He didn't leave. Just stood there, towel around his neck, watching me with those impossible gray eyes.

"Something else, Chief Drake?"

"You really going to do this?" His voice dropped, rough. "Close a station that's served this town for sixty years?"

"I'm going to enforce regulations that keep firefighters alive." Cool. Neutral. "If your station can't meet minimum standards—"

"Minimum standards written by people who've never fought a real fire."

"Written by people who've studied every fire death in the last fifty years." Heat crept into my voice. "Written in the blood of firefighters who died because someone decided rules didn't apply to them."

A muscle jumped in his jaw. "We're not cutting corners."

"You're operating with insufficient equipment and personnel. Those aren't suggestions. They're requirements."

"Requirements that cost money this town doesn't have." He stepped closer. The scent of him—salt and smoke—made my pulse kick. "You want to tell Mayor Thompson to raise taxes? Explain to the council why the fire department matters more than fixing the school roof? Be my guest. I'll watch."

"That's not my job."

"No. Your job is checking boxes." Another step. "My job is making sure my crew comes home. I've been doing it for seventeen years."

"Seventeen years of luck."

"Skill." His eyes flashed. "But you wouldn't know the difference, would you? Probably never been inside a working fire in your life."

The air left my lungs. For one horrible second I was back, smoke choked me—phantom but real. Derek s voice crackled through memory's static..

My hands clenched. Something must have shown on my face because Mason's expression shifted. The anger scftened into something that looked almost like concern.

"Inspector—"

His phone rang.

Mason glanced at the screen, and irritation mixed with something warmer. He answered, turning the phone so I looked at the phone.

A leaner, lighter version of Mason grinned from the screen. Same gunmetal, but with laugh lines instead of command. "Hey, big brother. How's—" He stopped, clearly seeing me. His grin widened. "Well. You didn't mention the state inspector was gorgeous."

Heat flooded my face. I turned to my laptop.

"Wyatt. I'm busy."

"I can see that. Does she know you only own two shirts?"

"Goodbye, Wyatt."

"Come on, introduce me." Wyatt leaned toward his camera. "I'm Wyatt Drake, ma'am. The charming brother."

"Inspector Zhang," I said without turning.

"Beautiful name. You single?"

Mason ended the call.

The silence felt thick enough to drown in. I kept my eyes on my screen, hyperaware of him behind me. My neck burned where I imagined his gaze.

Stop. This is a job. Two weeks, then gone.

"He's always like that," Mason said finally. "Ignore him."

"Already forgotten."

A lie. I'd remember the way Mason's ears had gone red. The way he'd shut down his brother's flirting, protective and embarrassed.

Human. Real.

I needed him to be the obstacle. The stubborn chief I could write up and walk away from.

The station alarm shattered the quiet—a blaring shriek that sent adrenaline knifing through my veins.

Mason's transformation was instant. The man disappeared. The chief emerged.

He was out the door before I could blink, voice already barking orders. "Javi! Thompson! Structure fire, 247 Main! Full turnout, two minutes!"

I stood frozen, listening to organized chaos. Boots pounding. Engines starting. Radio chatter, clipped and efficient.

Then silence.

I pulled up the dispatch information. 247 Main Street. The Morrison Building—three stories, mixed use. Built in 1962, wood frame with brick facade. Outdated electrical. Fire escapes flagged for repair twice.

People could be trapped.

I grabbed my tablet and stood. Stopped.

You're an inspector. You don't do this anymore.

But I couldn't just sit here. Couldn't wait and wonder and hope they came back.

Not again.

I clipped my radio to my belt and walked into the empty bay.

The engines were gone. The bay doors stood open to afternoon sun.

Somewhere downtown, Mason and his undermanned crew were running into a burning building with equipment I'd flagged as insufficient.

My inspection. My report.

If someone didn't come home—

I got in my SUV and drove toward the smoke rising over Main Street, hands white-knuckled on the wheel.

Professional due diligence, I told myself.

But my hands were shaking and I knew exactly what I was really afraid of.

Ashes and Adrenaline

♥

The engine screamed through downtown. Gray-black smoke boiled from second-floor windows. Flames licked the window frames. Mrs. Smith stood on the sidewalk in her apron, her face a mask of terror.

"My grandson!" She grabbed my coat. "Tommy—he's upstairs! He was doing homework, I told him I'd be right back—"

"We've got him." I squeezed her shoulder, a promise that felt heavy as lead. I had to deliver.

My crew moved like the well-oiled machine I'd built them into. As Javi and I geared up, a black SUV pulled into the lot.

Lily Zhang emerged, tablet in hand, radio already clipped to her belt. She'd changed into dark jeans and a departmental polo that did nothing to hide the athletic lines of her body. Her focus was absolute, her gaze locked on the fire, assessing. It was the look of a professional, and it was ridiculously, infuriatingly attractive.

"Inspector," I grunted. "Stay back."

"I'm required to observe operations." Her voice was clipped. She took up a position near the pump panel, a silent, judging shadow.

Fine. Let her watch.

We made entry. Heat slammed into me like opening an oven door to hell, the smoke a choking blanket. The old building groaned around us, the sound of stressed timber a warning.

"Fire department! Call out!"

Only the roar of the flames answered. We pushed up the stairs, sweeping the rooms. Empty. The fire was spreading fast, running through the walls. We were running out of time.

"Chief Drake." Lily's voice cut through the radio. Clear. Precise. No panic. "Building records show a false ceiling concealing an attic crawl space. Fire's in that void."

I stopped. My thermal camera confirmed it—a river of heat running just above our heads.

"The northeast bedroom," she continued. "Check the closet."

I didn't question it. We moved to the second bedroom, yanked open the closet door. A small shape huddled in the corner.

"Got him!" I scooped the boy up. He was light in my arms, his face smudged with soot, but he gave a weak cough. Breathing.

"Chief, we need to move!" Javi's voice was tight. "Structure's compromised."

Lily's voice again, a lifeline of calm in the chaos. "Northeast stairwell is clear. Backdoor exit through the kitchen—avoid the main stairs."

We followed her route. Seconds after we cleared the doorway, the ceiling behind us collapsed with a thunderous crash that shook the building to its foundation.

We emerged into clean air and the welcome chaos of arriving mutual aid. I handed Tommy to the paramedics, watched until he started crying for his grandmother.

Alive.

I bent over, hands on my knees, sucking in air that didn't taste like death. The adrenaline crash hit, my hands starting to shake. I scanned the scene, found Lily by her SUV. She stood rigid, her tablet clutched to her chest. As she watched them load Tommy into the ambulance, she let out a breath she'd clearly been holding, a small, shaky exhalation.

I crossed to her, my turnout coat still smoking slightly. "Where'd you learn to fight fires?"

She blinked, the professional mask sliding back into place. "Building codes. Public records."

"That wasn't a public record. That was a save." I stepped closer. "You've been inside."

"I'm an inspector, Chief Drake," she said, but her voice wasn't quite steady. "This is my job."

"Chief!" Mrs. Smith appeared and threw her arms around Lily. Not me. Lily. "Thank you, thank you. My Tommy..."

Lily froze, her arms stiff at her sides. Her eyes filled, and she blinked hard, her throat working. "I didn't... The chief and his crew did the work." She gently extracted herself from the hug, her composure fragile.

The bureaucrat vanished. The enemy disappeared. Only the ghost remained.

Haunted by something I didn't understand.

***

Midnight found the station quiet, the crew crashed in their bunks. I was too wired to sleep, the near-miss replaying in my head. I found her in my office, still working, the glow of the laptop turning her skin pale. A stray strand of black hair had escaped her bun and lay against her cheek.

Her coffee mug was empty.

I went to the kitchen, made a fresh pot, and brought her a cup without a word.

She looked up, surprised, as I set it on the desk.

"You saved time in there tonight," I said, leaning against the door-frame. "Maybe saved us, too."

"I was doing my job." She wrapped both hands around the mug, absorbing its warmth.

"That was something else."

Silence stretched, thick with unspoken questions.

"You've fought fires before," I said quietly. "What happened?"

Her hands stilled. I expected a wall, a sharp retort. Instead, she just looked down at the mug. "Nothing relevant to this audit," she said, her voice barely a whisper.

She didn't tell me to leave. She took a sip of the coffee.

It was enough for now.

"Get some sleep, Inspector," I said. "Tomorrow I'll show you why we do things our way."

The corner of her mouth twitched. Not a smile, but the ghost of one. It transformed her face, softening the hard lines into something vulnerable.

"I'll be ready, Chief."

I turned and walked away before I did something stupid, like ask her to stay. Not just in the office, but to stay. I paused at the door and glanced back.

She was staring at her screen, but she wasn't working. She was just holding the warm mug in both hands, her shoulders finally, fractionally, relaxed.

Coffee and Confessions

♥

I woke to the scratch of wool and the smell of industrial-strength laundry detergent. For a disoriented second, I didn't know where I was. The couch was stiff beneath me, the air in the office cool. Then it came back—the reports, the coffee, Mason's quiet exit, and my own failure to make it back to the hotel.

A standard-issue gray wool blanket, the kind found in every fire station in the country, was tucked around my shoulders. Someone had covered me.

Mason.

The thought was an unwelcome intrusion, a small, intimate act that breached my professional armor. I sat up, the blanket pooling in my lap. This was a complication. A kindness I hadn't asked for and didn't know how to categorize. I folded it with precise, sharp movements, creasing the edges, restoring order. I placed it on the corner of the desk, a neat, contained square. It meant nothing.

The rich smell of coffee and sizzling bacon pulled me from the office. I followed it down the hall to a common area, a combination kitchen and day room filled with the sounds of a station waking up.

And there he was.

Not Chief Drake, the infuriating, stubborn man who fought me on every regulation. This was Mason. He stood at an industrial-sized stove, a faded gray t-shirt stretched across his broad back, flipping pancakes with an easy rhythm. Luke and Javi sat at a long wooden table, nursing mugs, and the room was filled with the low murmur of conversation and the clink of ceramic on wood.

It was a family breakfast. And I was the auditor, the outsider, the threat.

The laughter died as I stepped into the room. Luke stared down at his plate. Javi gave me a cautious nod.

"Inspector." Mason's voice was different here. Quieter. He didn't turn around, but he gestured with his spatula toward the coffeepot. "Help yourself."

It was an invitation, not a command. An olive branch. To accept felt like a surrender. To refuse, an act of war. I poured a cup, my movements stiff, my spine rigid. I would observe, not participate.

"We do this every morning," Javi said, filling the awkward silence. "The Chief, here, he thinks cooking is a team-building exercise."

"It is," Mason said, sliding a stack of pancakes onto a plate. "A well-fed crew is a happy crew." He set the plate on the table, and his eyes—eyes the color of winter smoke—found mine. "Sit. Eat."

I hesitated. Sharing a meal was a concession, a crack in the wall I so carefully maintained. But every eye was on me. I sat at the far end of the table, my coffee mug a shield.

Mason put a plate in front of me before I could protest. The warmth from the ceramic seeped into the cold wood.

"You know," Luke piped up, his youthful earnestness cutting through the tension, "the council almost sold this place five years ago. Said it was too expensive to run."

"But the Chief wouldn't let 'em," Javi added, looking at Mason with a respect that was almost reverence. "Wrote the grants himself. Went door-to-door fundraising. Showed 'em all what this station means to Copper Ridge."

I looked at Mason, who was focused on pouring syrup, his ears turning a faint shade of red. He'd built this. Fought for it. It wasn't just a job; it was his life's work. My list of violations felt suddenly flimsy, a collection of words on a screen against the reality of this man's dedication.

After the plates were cleared, Mason grabbed his jacket. "Come on. I want to show you something."

He led me out into the crisp morning air and onto Main Street. We didn't talk about the inspection. He just walked, and I followed, a silent observer. He nodded to people, a quiet greeting that was always returned with a smile.

He stopped in front of the town bakery. "Morning, Mary," he called through the open door.

A woman with flour dusting her eyebrows beamed at him. "Mason! The usual?" She bustled out with a small paper bag. "And one for your friend. On the house." She pressed a warm, flaky pastry into my hand. The heat was a shock against my cold fingers. "This man and his crew saved my ovens last year. My whole livelihood." She patted Mason's arm. "Our guardian angel."

My cheeks burned. I was here to ground the guardian angel.

Mrs. Peterson waved from her flower box, calling out "God bless you and your crew, Mason." He nodded, his stride never breaking.

These weren't statistics. They were faces. Names. Livelihoods and lives. Each one was a testament against the cold logic of my report.

"My preliminary report's due Friday," I said as we turned back toward the station. The words came out sharper than intended.

Mason's hand brushed mine—accidental or deliberate, I couldn't tell. "And?"

"And I have to make a recommendation. Conditional approval or operational review."

"Which means closure."

"Which means closure," I confirmed.

The silence stretched between us, heavy with implications neither of us wanted to voice.

By the time we walked back toward the station, the sun was higher in the sky, and the professional wall between us had crumbled into dust. He wasn't an obstacle anymore. He was the town's protector, its heartbeat. And I was the one holding the scalpel.

Our pace had slowed, the silence between us no longer a battleground but something comfortable. As we turned the corner onto the station's block, the back of his hand brushed against mine.

A jolt—sharp, electric, and utterly terrifying—shot up my arm. My entire nervous system screamed a warning. Too close. Too real. I snatched my hand back as if I'd been burned. He did the same. Our eyes met for a split second, and in his, I saw the same shock, the same silent acknowledgment that a line had been crossed.

I didn't know what to do with it. With him.

I didn't have to.

The station alarm blared, a piercing shriek that sliced through the morning quiet, shattering the moment.

Mason was already moving, his entire posture changing from the relaxed man I'd just walked with back to the chief. He was all focus, all authority.

"Stay here," he ordered over his shoulder as he broke into a run.

The old Lily, the inspector who lived by rules and regulations, would have obeyed. But the woman who had just seen the faces of the people he protected, the firefighter who still lived somewhere deep inside me, couldn't.

I ran after him, my heart beating a frantic, familiar rhythm against my ribs.

"Not a chance."

Baptism By Flame

♥

The smoke was a black pillar against the blue Colorado sky, visible from five miles out. By the time we arrived, the warehouse was a roaring beast, devouring itself from the inside out. Flames shot through the roof, and the heat hit me through the windshield like a physical blow.

"Two workers, shipping and receiving, unaccounted for," Javi relayed from dispatch. "Mutual aid is rolling from Fairplay. ETA twenty minutes."

Twenty minutes.

Inside that inferno, twenty minutes was a death sentence.

I killed the engine. "Javi, you're on the pump. Luke, you're with me. Search and rescue."

"Chief, the roof structure is bowstring truss," Javi said, his eyes on the fire. "It's not gonna hold."

"We're not waiting for it to fall." I started gearing up. Every second counted.

A car door slammed. Lily strode toward me, her face pale but her eyes blazing.

"What are you doing?" she demanded.

"My job." I pulled my hood over my head.

"You can't go in there. Your crew is too small. The risk assessment—"

"The risk assessment is two men are going to burn to death if I listen to a damn rulebook!" I turned to face her fully. "You want to stand here and quote regulations? Fine. But I'm going in."

She grabbed my arm. Her touch was a shock, even through the thick material of my coat. "This is exactly the kind of risk that gets people killed, Mason. I've seen it."

Her voice cracked on the last word. For a split second, the inspector was gone, replaced by a woman haunted by ghosts.

"And sitting here definitely gets those workers killed," I said, my voice dropping. "Sometimes the book doesn't save lives, Lily. People do."

I pulled my arm free and didn't look back.

***

The heat inside was a solid wall.

The world dissolved into a roaring, blinding hell. Smoke and flame. The groan of twisting metal. The crack of timber giving way. Luke stayed tight on my six as we pushed deeper, following the hose line.

"Fire department! Call out!"

Then, a weak shout from our right.

We found them huddled under a steel desk. Two young men. One with a nasty gash on his forehead. Both terrified but alive.

"We're getting you out of here," I yelled, pulling one to his feet while Luke grabbed the other.

We turned to retrace our path.

The concrete floor bucked beneath my boots. A section of the roof fifty feet ahead came down in a shower of sparks and flaming debris, cutting off our exit.

We were trapped.

"Mayday, Mayday, Mayday." My heart slammed against my ribs. "Engine Five to Command. We are trapped. Two firefighters, two civilians. South side, shipping area. Exit is blocked."

The radio crackled.

I expected Javi's voice.

I got hers.

"Command to Engine Five, I copy your Mayday." Lily's voice was unnaturally calm. Steady. Clear. The voice of someone who'd done this before, who'd led crews through hell and brought them home. "Chief, I have the schematics. Acknowledge."

"Go for Engine Five."

"There's a service corridor twenty feet to your west. Behind a roll-up metal door. It should lead you to the exterior wall on the C-side. Can you locate it?"

I scanned the smoke-filled darkness with my thermal imager. A cooler rectangle appeared on the wall. The door.

"I see it. Manual chain hoist."

"Understood. Get it open."

The chain was searing hot. The smoke thick enough to choke on. Luke and I threw our weight against it, muscles screaming, lungs burning. The civilians coughed and gagged behind us.

For a terrifying minute, it wouldn't budge.

Then, with a scream of protesting metal, it began to rise.

"We're through!" I yelled into the radio, shoving the workers into the corridor.

"Keep moving north, Chief," Lily's voice guided us. That calm, steady presence over the radio. "Exit door should be forty feet ahead on your left."

We stumbled through the narrow passage, half-carrying the injured men.

Just as my hand found the push bar on the exit door, the main roof of the warehouse collapsed with a deafening, final groan. The backdraft sucked the air from the corridor, pulling us out the door and onto the gravel lot behind the building.

We fell in a heap. Gasping. Coughing. Sucking in the clean, cool air. Alive.

Paramedics swarmed us, but my eyes searched the chaos.

I saw her then. Standing by the command vehicle. Her tablet lowered. Our eyes met across the fireground.

I pushed myself to my feet and walked toward her, stripping off my helmet and gloves. The world seemed to narrow to the space between us.

She met me halfway.

Her professional mask was completely gone. Her eyes, wide with a fear that was raw and real, scanned me from head to toe.

"You could've died," she whispered, her voice rough.

Her hands came up. Touching my face. Her fingers traced my jaw, checking for injuries I didn't have. Her touch was trembling but firm. An anchor in the adrenaline-fueled storm.

All the anger, all the fight between us, evaporated in that single, unguarded touch.

"But I didn't," I said, my voice hoarse. I covered her hand with mine, pressing it against my cheek. The soot on my skin smudged against her palm. "Thanks to you."

Her breath hitched.

Her gaze dropped to my lips.

The space between us crackled. Charged with the life we'd almost lost. I leaned in. She leaned in. The fire, the noise, the chaos—it all faded away.

"Chief!" Javi's voice cut through the moment like a physical blow. "You good?"

We jumped apart like we'd been burned.

Lily snatched her hand back, her cheeks flushing. The inspector was back, her walls slamming into place.

But it was too late.

I'd seen behind them. I'd felt her fear, her relief, her need.

And I knew, with a certainty that shook me to my core, that nothing between us would ever be the same.

Three A.M. Truths

♥

The station clock read eleven-seventeen. I'd been staring at the same regulation paragraph for ten minutes, the words blurring into meaningless shapes on my laptop screen. Three days. Seventy-two hours since I'd arrived in Copper Ridge, and my entire world, once governed by neat lines and regulations, had been knocked off its grid.

I pulled off my reading glasses and rubbed my eyes. The office felt too quiet, too small. Through the window, I saw the apparatus bay, the gleaming engines sitting silent in the darkness. Somewhere in the building, the night crew slept. Mason had left hours ago—or so I thought.

Three days.

I typed another note into my report, something about equipment rotation schedules, but my mind kept circling back to that moment this morning. His hand brushing mine. The jolt of electricity that had shot straight through my carefully constructed armor. The way he'd looked at me, storm-colored eyes wide with the same shock I'd felt.

This wasn't me. I didn't do this—didn't let people in, didn't feel things this fast, this hard. I was Inspector Zhang, all sharp edges and regulations. Not the woman whose pulse kicked into overdrive every time Mason Drake walked into a room.

The door opened. No knock, because of course not. Mason never knocked.

"Thought you'd gone home." I kept my eyes on the screen, fingers moving across the keyboard. Professional. Controlled.

"Thought you had too." He set a mug on the desk beside me. The smell of fresh coffee filled the space between us. "But your car's still here, and the light's on, so..."

I glanced at the mug. Black, no sugar. He'd been paying attention.

"These equipment logs won't review themselves." The words felt automatic on my tongue, a familiar shield. The truth was, the logs were done. Had been for an hour. But the thought of my sterile hotel room—the too-firm bed, the silence that let the memories in—made the worn vinyl of this office chair feel like a sanctuary.

Mason didn't take his chair behind the desk He dropped into the visitor's chair, the one right across from me. Closer. The worn denim of his jeans was a stark contrast to my own pressed slacks. He'd traded his turnout gear for a simple gray henley, the soft fabric doing a poor job of hiding the solid muscle of his chest and shoulders. His hair was damp at the temples, and the clean scent of soap and pine cut through the stale office air, a combination that was entirely too distracting. My fingers tensed on my keyboard.

"We make a good team." He leaned back, studying me. "Today, at the warehouse. You and me."

My fingers stilled on the keyboard. "I was just doing my job."

"No." His voice dropped, that gravelly tone that sent a tremor straight through my center. "You were doing more than that. The way you handled those schematics, guided us out... That wasn't from any manual."

I forced myself to meet his eyes. "I told you. I read a lot."

"Lily." Just my name, but the way he said it—soft, knowing—made my chest tight. "You fight fires like someone who's been burned."

The words hung in the air between us. My hand moved to my shoulder, an unconscious gesture, fingers finding the edge of the scar hidden beneath my sweater.

"Leave it alone, Mason."

"Can't do that." He leaned forward, elbows on his knees. "You saved my crew today. You've been saving us since you got here, whether you want to admit it or not. But you look at fire like it's going to turn on you. Like you're waiting for something terrible to happen."

"Something terrible always happens." My voice was tight, the words clipping off. "That's why regulations exist. To prevent—"

"To prevent what?" His eyes searched mine. "What happened to you?"

I should have stood up, walked out, maintained the wall between us. Instead, I heard myself say, "I was twenty-eight."

Mason went still, like he knew any movement might spook me into silence.

"Twenty-eight." I pulled my hair free, needing something to do with my hands. Black strands fell around my shoulders.

"Chicago?"

I nodded. "Station 19. Made lieutenant young—too young, most said." My fingers twisted in the loose hair. "But my crew trusted me."

My hands clenched. "Apartment fire. Family trapped on three." I pressed my palms against my eyes. "Building was supposed to be empty. Renovation. But squatters had moved in."

"The roof."

Mason's expression shifted. He'd already put it together.

"Bowstring truss?"

"Parallel chord." My voice dropped to barely above a whisper. "Looked stable. Fire had been burning in the cockloft for hours before we arrived." I stood abruptly, crossing to the window. Distance helped. "We found the family. Got them to the stairwell."

My reflection stared back—pale, haunted.

"Then the ceiling started dropping.'

The words stuck in my throat. Mason moved his chair closer, until our knees almost touched.

"The ceiling started dropping chunks. Not just debris—whole sections of the truss system. We needed to move fast, needed to—" I couldn't speak for a moment.

"I froze. Standing there in the middle of hell, my crew looking to me for orders, and I couldn't move. Couldn't think. Couldn't breathe."

"Lily—"

"Derek took over." The name was a physical weight in my mouth, thick and bitter. "My partner. He'd been on the job fifteen years, knew what to do. Got everyone moving, got us toward the exit. But the structure kept failing, and someone had to hold the beam that was blocking our path while the others got through."

My voice broke. Mason's hand moved toward mine, stopped just short of touching.

"He was my fiancé." The confession shattered my control, and the words started tumbling out, one over the other. "We were getting married in three months—the venue, the flowers, it was all planned—and he stayed behind to hold that beam. He told me to go. 'Go, Lily. Now.' That was the last thing he said."

Tears burned my eyes. I blinked hard, refusing to let them fall.

"The beam gave way twenty seconds after we cleared the building. Twenty seconds." A harsh, humorless sound escaped my throat. "The department called him a hero. The newspapers wrote about his sacrifice. But I know the truth. If I hadn't frozen, if I'd kept my head, we could have found another way. He died because I failed."

"That's not—"

"Three other firefighters were injured getting out. One has permanent lung damage. Can't work anymore." I met Mason's eyes. "Their families sued the department. Settled out of court, but everyone knew it was my fault. The lieutenant who choked when it mattered."

The office felt too small, the air too thick. I stood, pacing to the window. My reflection stared back—pale, haunted, nothing like the put-together inspector I pretended to be.

"I quit the next day. Couldn't trust myself to lead anyone anywhere ever again. Moved to inspection because rules don't require courage. Just compliance."

Mason's chair creaked. His footsteps crossed the room, stopped just behind me. I felt the heat of him, close but not touching.

"You didn't freeze at the warehouse today."

"That was different."

"How?"

"I wasn't inside. Wasn't responsible for—"

"For my life? For Luke's?" His reflection appeared beside mine in the window. "You were giving orders, Lily. Leading us out. That was all you."

"Stop." I turned to face him, back against the wall. Bad idea. He was too close, filling up all the space, making it hard to think. "You don't understand. I haven't felt anything for two years. Nothing. I've been walking around like a ghost, going through the motions, and that was fine. Safe. Then I come here, and you—"

I broke off, heat flooding my cheeks.

"Me what?" He moved closer, one hand bracing against the wall beside my head.

"Three days." The words came out barely above a whisper. "I've known you three days, and you're already under my skin. Nearly kissed you at a fire scene, for God's sake. That s not normal. That's not me."

"Feels pretty normal to me." His other hand came up, fingers barely grazing my cheek. "Crazy, maybe. Fast, definitely. But normal? Yeah."

"How can you say that?"

"Because I've dated women for months and never felt what I feel when you walk into a room." His thumb traced my cheekbone. "Like everything suddenly makes sense. Like I've been waiting for you without knowing it."

"Mason..."

"I know it's fast. I know it's probably the worst timing in the world. But when you know, you know. And Lily?" He tipped my chin up, forcing me to meet his eyes. "I know."

The distance between us evaporated. His mouth found mine, soft at first, tentative, like he was giving me room to pull away. But I was done pulling away. Done being careful. Done being a ghost.

I kissed him back, and gentle went out the window.

His hands tangled in my hair. Mine fisted in his shirt, pulling him closer. The kiss deepened, weeks of tension exploding in a rush of heat and need. He tasted like coffee and something darker, something that made me want to climb inside him and never leave.

"God, Lily." He lifted me onto the desk, stepping between my legs. Papers scattered. My laptop slid sideways. I didn't care.

His mouth moved to my neck, and I forgot how to breathe. My legs wrapped around his waist, pulling him closer, needing more. His hands skimmed my sides, thumbs brushing the underside of my breasts through my sweater.

"Mason—"

He kissed me again, swallowing whatever I'd been about to say. Probably for the best, since I had no idea what that was. My hands found skin where his shirt had ridden up, the muscles of his back flexing under my touch.

This was insane. Reckless. Everything I'd sworn I'd never do again. I didn't care.

His mouth found that spot below my ear that made me gasp. My back arched, pressing closer, and he groaned against my throat. The sound shot straight through me, pooling low in my belly.

"Been wanting to do this since you walked into Copper Ridge." His teeth scraped my collarbone. "All ice and regulations and those damn shoes that shouldn't be sexy but—"

The alarm shrieked through the station.

We froze, breathing hard, his forehead pressed against mine.

"Medical emergency, 1847 Pine Ridge Road. Possible cardiac arrest."

"Damn it." Mason pulled back, chest heaving. His hair stood up where I'd run my fingers through it. His mouth was swollen from kissing me. "I have to—"

"Go." I slid off the desk, legs unsteady. "Go."

He headed for the door, then turned back. Two strides, and he was kissing me again, hard and fast and full of promise.

"This isn't over."

Then he was gone, boots pounding down the hall toward the apparatus bay.

I sank into the chair, fingers pressed to my lips. They felt swollen, sensitive. A frantic energy buzzed under my skin, as if every nerve ending had been woken from a long sleep.

Three days. I'd known Mason Drake for three days, and I'd just let him—wanted him to—

"Maybe it should be," I whispered to my own haunted reflection in the dark window. "This is too fast. Too much."

But even as I said it, even as I tried to rebuild those careful walls, I knew the truth.

It was already too late.

I was already in trouble.

The Weight of Want

♥

Four-thirty in the morning. The sun was still a rumor behind the mountains as I killed the engine in the station lot. Sleep was a joke. For three hours, I'd seen nothing but Lily behind my eyes. Her back against my office wall. My name a gasp on her lips. I'd punched my pillow twice before giving up, the smell of her still clinging to my shirt from last night, a ghost in the cab of my truck. I needed to burn it off.

The station sat quiet, only the overnight crew inside. I bypassed the main entrance and headed straight for the training yard, needing to burn off this restless energy before she arrived.

My phone buzzed as I finished my second cup of terrible station coffee. Wyatt.

Wyatt: *So... that inspector. She settling in okay?*

I stared at the text, suspicious. Wyatt never just checked in about station business.

Mason: *Why do you care?*

Wyatt: *You sounded different on that video call. Figured I should know who's got my brother tied up in knots. Where'd she come from before Denver?*

Mason: *Before that, Chicago.*

Three dots appeared, then disappeared. Then appeared again.

Wyatt: *You know me. Can't help being nosy. Chicago's a big department - she must've seen some serious action there.*

Mason: *She knows what she's doing.*

Wyatt: *Just looking out for you, big brother, and your station.*

I set the phone down, that uneasy feeling settling in my gut. Wyatt was never just curious.

--

Bare knuckles met worn leather, the impact jarring up my arm. Again. The sting across my skin was a welcome distraction, a clean pain to blot out the messy one in my chest. Lily. Another strike. Her lips. Another. Her scent. The bag groaned, swinging on its chain. It wasn't enough.

This wasn't like me. I didn't do instant. Didn't believe in lightning strikes and love at first sight and all that romantic garbage Wyatt used to justify his string of one-night stands. I was the steady one. The planner. The one who thought things through.

Except Lily had walked into my fire station with her designer heels and her clipboard, and every carefully constructed wall I'd built had started cracking.

"You're here early."

I spun, heart hammering. She stood in the doorway, backlit by the rising sun. It caught the edges of her dark hair, making the individual strands look like live wires. She'd traded her usual power suit for department-issue workout gear—navy pants and a gray t-shirt with

CRFD printed across the chest. The clothes were too big for her frame, rolled at the cuffs and waist.

She looked soft. Touchable. Dangerous.

"Couldn't sleep." The words came out rougher than intended.

"Me either." She stepped into the shed, and I caught her shampoo smell—something floral that didn't match the industrial setting. Her gaze dropped to my hands. "You're bleeding."

I looked down. Split knuckles, blood seeping. Hadn't noticed.

"It's nothing."

She moved closer, close enough that I saw the faint shadows under her eyes. She'd been awake too, then. Thinking about last night. About that kiss that had knocked the foundation out from under me.

"We should talk about—"

"We should train." I grabbed a towel, wrapped it around my hand. "You said you're rusty. Can't have an inspector who can't handle basic equipment."

Her jaw tensed. "I can handle equipment just fine."

"Prove it."

The challenge sparked something in her eyes. Good. Competition was safer than conversation. Physical activity was safer than standing here, remembering how she'd felt in my arms.

Twenty minutes later, we stood in the training yard with the morning sun warming the concrete. I'd laid out the basics—hoses, couplings, ladder sections. Standard stuff every firefighter should know in their sleep.

"Hose deployment first." I demonstrated the proper stance. "Feet shoulder-width apart, weight balanced. You're fighting water pressure, not just carrying equipment."

She mimicked my position, and I bit back a groan. Her focus, the determined set of her shoulders, the way she bit her lower lip when concentrating—everything about her pulled at me.

"Like this?"

"Almost." I moved behind her, hands hovering. "Can I—?"

Yes."

My hands settled on her waist, adjusting her stance. The contact sent electricity racing up my arms. She tensed, then relaxed into my grip.

"Lower." My voice had gone rough again. "Bend your knees more."

She adjusted, and my hands followed the movement. Through the thin fabric of her shirt, I felt her breathing quicken.

"Better?" Her voice had a breathless quality that made me want to press closer, to feel more than just the suggestion of her body against mine.

"Better." I stepped back, putting necessary distance between us. "Now, coupling attachment. Speed matters, but accuracy matters more."

She grabbed the brass coupling, muscle memory taking over. Her movements were sure, practiced, only slightly slower than they would have been two years ago. The hose locked into place with a satisfying click.

"Good. Again."

She repeated the motion, faster this time. Then again. Each repetition brought back more of her confidence, more of the firefighter she'd been before Chicago broke her.

"Ladder raise next." I positioned the twenty-four-foot extension ladder flat on the ground. "Remember, it's about leverage, not strength."

She moved to the base, planted her feet, and began the raise. Halfway up, the ladder wobbled. I stepped in, hands bracketing hers on the rungs, helping guide it vertical.

"I've got it." But she didn't pull away from my touch.

"I know you do." My chest pressed against her back as we steadied the ladder together. "You've always had it. You just forgot for a while."

She turned her head, and suddenly her mouth was inches from mine. Morning light caught the gold flecks in her dark eyes. The same eyes that had been haunted yesterday now held heat.

"Mason—"

"Chief! You starting training without us?"

We jerked apart. Javi stood at the edge of the training yard, coffee in hand, knowing grin on his face. Luke bounced beside him, eager as a puppy.

"Just getting an early start." I took two more steps back, creating professional distance.

"Sure you were." Javi's grin widened. "Inspector, you joining us for regular morning drills?"

"I..." Lily smoothed her hands down her pants, a nervous gesture. "If that's acceptable."

"More than acceptable." Javi raised his coffee cup in salute. "Always good to have skilled hands. Right, Chief?"

Heat crawled up my neck. "Let's run ladder drills. Thompson, you're on belay."

The morning progressed in controlled chaos. Lily fell into the drill routine as if she'd never left, her body remembering what her mind had tried to forget. She moved through the exercises with increasing confidence—hose lays, ladder raises, search patterns.

But the real torture was the thousand small moments of contact. Adjusting her grip on the ax. Spotting her on the ladder climb. Our hands brushing as we coiled hose. Each touch was professional, necessary, and it was maddening.

By the time we finished, the sun had climbed high and everyone was drenched in sweat. The crew headed inside for showers and lunch. Lily lingered, helping me store equipment.

"You were good out there." I hung the last section of hose to dry.

"I was adequate."

"You were good. Own it."

She pulled the elastic from her ponytail, dark hair spilling over her shoulders. The gesture was unconscious, natural, and it made me ache to touch her.

"About last night—"

"Don't." The word came out harsher than intended. "Don't say it was a mistake."

"It was unprofessional."

I turned to face her fully. "It was honest."

"Mason, I'm leaving in ten days."

"Nine." The correction slipped out before I could stop it. I'd been counting. "Nine days, sixteen hours, and some change."

Her breath hitched. "You're counting."

"Been counting since you told me you'd leave." I moved closer, drawn by a force I couldn't name. "Can't stop thinking about it. Can't stop thinking about you."

"This is crazy." But she didn't back away. "Four days. We've known each other for four days."

"Feels like longer."

"That's what scares me." Her voice dropped to barely above a whisper. "I don't do this. I won't lose control."

"Maybe you're tired of being in control all the time."

Before she could respond, Luke's voice carried across the yard. "Chief! Javi says we're hitting the Grizzly tonight. You in?"

The moment shattered. Lily stepped back, walls sliding back into place.

"Tonight?" My voice was aimed at Luke, but my eyes were locked on her.

"Yeah! Band's playing. Whole crew's going." Luke appeared around the corner, grinning. "Inspector, you should come too. You're practically crew now."

Lily hesitated. I saw the war in her eyes—professional distance versus the connections she was building here.

"Come." The word was a gravelly command, rougher than I'd meant. I cleared my throat. "The crew wants you there."

"Just the crew?"

Luke had already jogged back inside, leaving us alone again.

"No." The word was quiet, but it felt like a confession. "Not just the crew."

***

Neon beer signs bled red and blue onto scarred wooden tables at The Grizzly. On a small stage, a local band butchered a passable 'Sweet Home Alabama'. It was loud, crowded, and perfect. Half the town had shown up, crowding around scarred wooden tables and leaving the small dance floor mostly empty.

Lily had changed into jeans and a black tank top, her hair loose around her shoulders. She sat wedged between Javi and Luke at our usual corner booth, nursing a beer and laughing at Luke's terrible jokes. I watched her laugh at something Luke said, her head thrown back, the harsh fluorescent lights of the bar catching on her teeth. The rigid line of her shoulders was gone. The woman who'd walked into my life four days ago wouldn't have known how to laugh like that. This version of her was... real. And a hell of a lot more dangerous.

I couldn't stop watching her.

"You're being obvious." Javi appeared at my elbow by the bar, ordering another round.

"Don't know what you mean."

"Right." He collected his beers. "Just ask her to dance already. Before you burn a hole through her with all that staring."

The band switched to something slower, couples moving onto the dance floor. Our eyes met across the room, and the air between us went tight, like a rope pulled taut.

I crossed to the booth before I could talk myself out of it. "Dance with me."

Luke started to say something, but Javi elbowed him quiet.

Lily hesitated, fingers tightening on her beer bottle. "I don't really dance."

"Neither do I."

That earned a small smile. "Liar. I saw the trophies in your office. High school dance team?"

"My mother's." I extended my hand. "She made me learn. Said every man should know how to properly hold a woman."

The words hung between us, loaded with meaning. Lily set down her beer and placed her hand in mine.

The dance floor was dimly lit, other couples creating a buffer of privacy. I pulled her close, one hand on her lower back, the other holding hers. She fit against me perfectly, her head reaching just to my shoulder.

"This is crazy." Her breath warmed my neck.

"So you keep saying."

"Because it's true." She pulled back enough to meet my eyes. "I plan. I analyze. I make spreadsheets before buying a coffee maker."

"How's that working out for you?"

"It was working fine until you."

We swayed to the music, bodies pressed close enough that I felt every breath she took. Her fingers grasping my shoulder.

"I can't stop thinking about last night." The confession came out soft, meant only for me. "About that kiss. About how much I wanted..." She trailed off, cheeks flushing even in the dim light.

"Tell me."

"Mason."

"Tell me what you wanted."

She was quiet for so long I thought she wouldn't answer. Then, barely audible over the music: "Everything. I wanted everything."

The song ended, but neither of us moved. Around us, couples separated, returned to their tables, but we stood frozen in our bubble.

"Let's get out of here."

I led her through the crowd, ignoring Javi's knowing look, Luke's confused expression. The parking lot was cool after the warmth of the bar, mountain air sharp with pine.

We made it three steps before I had her against the side of the building, my mouth on hers.

This kiss was different from last night—deeper, desperate, tinged with decision. Her hands fisted in my shirt, pulling me closer. I pressed her into the brick wall, needing to feel all of her, needing to climb inside this moment and live there.

"Come home with me." The words came out rough against her mouth.

She pulled back, breathing hard. "If I do this, I don't know if I can leave in nine days."

I kissed her again, swallowing her protests. When we broke apart, her eyes had gone dark.

"One night." Her voice shook. "Just... one night to get this out of our systems."

We both knew she was lying. One night would never be enough. But I'd take what she'd give.

"One night." I agreed to the lie.

She looked at me for a long moment, something shifting in her expression. Then she took my hand and headed for my truck.

"Let's go."

Surrender

♥

The truck engine ticked as it cooled in the darkness. Mason's hand rested on the gear shift between us, his knuckles still split from this morning's punching bag. Here we sat in his driveway, about to go into his cabin like this was normal. Like my entire body wasn't screaming that this was too fast, too much, too everything.

"You okay?" Mason's voice cut through the silence. Not demanding. Just checking.

I turned to look at him. Dashboard lights carved shadows across his jaw. The stubble there would scrape my skin. Not if. When. Because despite the panic clawing at my ribs, I wasn't getting out of this truck without him.

His thumb moved, brushing across my knuckles where my hand gripped my thigh. "Want me to take you back?"

His shoulders were set, his body held carefully still. He would drive me back to the hotel right now if I asked. No questions, no pressure, no guilt.

And the sincerity in that offer, the complete lack of pressure—that was the thing that broke through my panic.

"No." I unbuckled my seatbelt. "No, I don't want to go back."

We walked to his front door in silence. The cabin sat dark against the tree line, windows reflecting starlight. Pine needles crunched under our feet. The night air bit at my bare arms, raising goosebumps that had nothing to do with cold.

Mason unlocked the door, pushed it open, and stepped aside.

The cabin smelled like him—woodsmoke and pine and something clean that made senses reel. A few embers glowed in the stone fireplace. Leather furniture absorbed the darkness. Through the far windows, mountains cut jagged shapes against the stars.

"Lily." He stood in the doorway, blocking out the night. "We don't have to—"

I crossed the room in three strides and pulled his head down to mine, swallowing whatever responsible thing he was about to say. His hands came up to frame my face, thumbs stroking my cheekbones as he kissed me back. Gentle. Careful. Like I might break.

I didn't want careful.

I nipped at his bottom lip, pressed closer, let him feel how much I wanted this. His control cracked. A sound rumbled up from his chest as he walked me backward until my spine hit the wall. His mouth moved to my throat, teeth scraping the spot that made me gasp.

"Been thinking about this all day." His hands spanned my waist, thumbs brushing the strip of skin where my tank top had ridden up. "During training. At the bar. Every damn minute."

"Just today?" My voice came out breathless, teasing.

He pulled back to look at me, eyes gone dark. "Since you walked into my station like you owned it. Since you stood toe-to-toe with me and didn't back down." His thumb traced my bottom lip. "You've been driving me crazy for four days straight."

"Good." I tugged at his shirt. "That's only fair."

He reached for the hem of my tank top, paused. A question.

I raised my arms.

The fabric whispered away. Cool air hit my skin, and I fought the urge to cover myself. Not from modesty—from the scars. The ones that marked me as someone who'd failed when it mattered most.

Mason's gaze traveled over me, slow and thorough. When he found the burn scars on my left shoulder, the mangled skin that ran down my upper arm, his expression didn't change. No pity. No disgust. Just acceptance.

He lowered his head, pressed his lips to the worst of it. The twisted patch where falling debris had branded me. My throat closed.

"Beautiful." The word ghosted across damaged skin. "Every inch of you."

"Mason—"

"No." He straightened, hands framing my face again. "No hiding. Not from me."

His lips pushed against mine like he was trying to prove something. Like he could pour two years of my self-hatred down the drain with his mouth alone. Maybe he could. My knees went weak, and he caught me, lifting me like I weighed nothing.

"Bedroom?"

"Too far."

A laugh escaped him, muffled against my mouth as he lowered me to the couch. The leather was cool against my back, a sharp contrast to the heat of him settling over me. His weight pressed me into the cool leather, solid and real. He was everywhere—the heat of his skin, the scent of pine and soap, the strength in the hands bracketing my head. My breath hitched.

His mouth traced a path down my throat, across my collarbone. Each kiss was deliberate, unhurried, like he had all the time in the world to memorize every inch of exposed skin. When his lips found the hollow at the base of my throat, I arched into him, my fingers threading through his hair.

"Tell me what you want." His voice was rough against my skin. "Tell me what you need."

My hands slid under his shirt, fingers splaying across the hard planes of his back. The muscles there shifted under my touch, his body responding to every brush of my fingertips. I could feel his heart hammering against my chest, as wild and unsteady as my own.

"This," I whispered. "Just this."

His hands were careful as they explored—tracing my ribs, the curve of my waist, learning the shape of me through touch alone. When his palm settled over my racing heart, his fingers spread wide, I felt claimed in a way that had nothing to do with possession and everything to do with being truly seen.

We kissed until my lips felt swollen, until breathing became secondary to the taste of him. His stubble scraped my jaw, my neck, leaving a trail of heat in its wake. My hands mapped the geography of his shoulders, his arms, the solid warmth of him.

"Mason." His name was a plea, though I wasn't sure what I was asking for.

He seemed to understand anyway. His forehead pressed against mine, both of us breathing hard. "I've got you. Whatever you need. Whatever pace you want."

My hands stilled their exploration, resting against his shoulders. "Can we just... can we just stay like this? Kiss and touch and—" I swallowed hard. "I want you. God, I want you. But I'm not ready for more. Not tonight."

Relief flooded his expression so completely it made my eyes sting. "Yeah. Yes. Whatever you want, Lily."

"You're not disappointed?"

"Disappointed?" He shifted his weight, settling beside me on the couch so I could breathe, but keeping me tucked against his side. "I get to hold you all night. Get to fall asleep with you in my arms. There's nothing disappointing about that."

His fingers traced idle patterns on my shoulder, careful around the scarred tissue. Through the windows, stars wheeled overhead in their ancient dance.

"Tell me something," I said, my fingers finding the outline of a tattoo that disappeared under his shirt. "When did you know?"

"That I was in trouble?" His chest rumbled with quiet laughter. "Day one. You walked into my station in those shoes that shouldn't have been sexy but were, started cataloging violations, and I thought 'oh, I'm completely screwed.'""Day one?"

"Day one." He pressed a kiss to my temple. "You?"

I thought about it. The moment Mason had covered me with a blanket that first night I'd fallen asleep at my desk. The way he'd made coffee without being asked. How he'd looked at his crew—protective, proud, present.

"The blanket," I admitted. "That first night. Such a small thing, but nobody had done something like that for me in... I couldn't even remember. And I realized I was in serious trouble."

"So we were both doomed from the start."

"Completely doomed."

We stayed like that for hours—kissing, touching, learning each other in firelight. His mouth traced patterns across my collarbone. My fingers memorized the tattoos that marked his ribs, each one a story he told in fragments between kisses. The dates, the saves, the moments that had shaped him into the man who held me like I was something precious.

When exhaustion finally pulled us under, we were still tangled together, my head on his chest, his arms wrapped around me like a promise. The last thing I remembered was his lips against my hair and the steady rhythm of his heartbeat beneath my ear.

Safe. For the first time in two years, I felt completely, utterly safe.

***

"This is insane." I traced the dates tattooed down his ribs. Each one a fire, a save, a moment that mattered. "Literally insane."

"Best four days of my life."

I propped myself up to look at him. His hair stuck up in every direction.

Reality crept back in, cold and unwelcome. "What are we doing?"

"Living." His hand swept down my spine, making me shiver. "For the first time in two years, you're living." He caught my chin, made me meet his eyes. "I'm not asking you to stay forever. I'm asking you to stop thinking about leaving long enough to be here. With me. Now."

"And tomorrow?"

"We'll deal with tomorrow when it comes."

The simplicity of it terrified me. But lying here in his bed, skin to skin, his pulse steady under my palm—maybe simple was what I needed.

"Okay." I pressed my lips to the date over his heart. "Ten days. We make them count."

"Nine."

"You're really going to count down every day?"

"Every hour if you let me."

I laughed, the sound surprising me. When was the last time I'd laughed in bed with someone? When was the last time I'd felt this loose-limbed and safe?

"Tell me about this one." I touched the date on his shoulder. "2019."

"School fire. Got four kids out of a classroom. One of them was Javi's daughter." His fingers played with my hair. "That was the year after Dad's station almost got shut down. We'd just gotten the funding to stay open. First real save with the new equipment."

"And this one?" Lower on his ribs.

"Date I became chief. Youngest in the county's history." Pride colored his voice, then faded. "Also the day I realized I'd never leave Copper Ridge. Never have a life outside the station."

He was kissing me again, deep and slow, when his radio crackled from the nightstand.

"All stations, weather advisory. National Weather Service has issued a red flag warning for the next seven days. Winds gusting to 45 miles per hour expected. Humidity below 15 percent. Extreme fire danger for all counties."

Mason stilled above me. We both knew what that meant. The conditions were perfect for disaster.

The radio continued with technical details—wind speeds, humidity levels, temperature predictions. The dispatcher's voice was calm, professional, but I perceived the underlying tension. Every firefighter in the county would be on edge for the next week.

"Mason—"

"Not now." He turned the volume down but didn't switch it off. Always on duty, even here. Even now. "We have nine days. The weather can wait."

But the calm voice from the radio sliced through the warmth of the room. The air between us chilled, the bubble we'd been in popping into silence. Reality had crept in, reminding us both that the outside world wasn't going to pause just because we'd found each other.

He must have seen it in my face because he cupped my cheek, thumb stroking. "Hey. We're okay. Whatever comes, we handle it."

"Together?"

The word slipped out before I could stop it. Too much, too soon. But he just smiled, that rare full smile that transformed his face.

"Together."

Ghosts in the Daylight

♥

The morning sun cut through the fire station windows, glinting off the laptop screen where Lily was working. Four nights she'd woken up in my bed. Eight days since she'd walked in here and turned my world upside down. My crew pretended not to notice, but their grins gave them away.

"Chief, you've got that look again." Javi leaned against Engine One, coffee mug in hand.

"What look?"

"The one that says you're thinking about something that has nothing to do with hose maintenance."

Luke snorted from where he was checking equipment. "More like someone."

Lily glanced up from her laptop, a hint of pink coloring her cheeks. She'd commandeered the folding table near the day room, papers spread in neat stacks around her. Her hair was pulled back in that severe bun, but I knew how it looked loose across my pillows. Knew the sounds she made when I—

"See? That look." Javi shook his head. "You're gone, Jefe."

"Mind your business, Martinez."

"Hard to do when the air between you two could start a damn fire."

Lily's fingers paused on her keyboard. She didn't look up, but the corner of her mouth twitched. That small almost-smile did something to my insides. Made them expand and contract at the same time.

"For what it's worth," Luke said, coiling hose with exaggerated focus, "we think it's great. You and the inspector. She's good for you."

"She has a name, Thompson."

"Right. Sorry. Lily's good for you."

The kid was right. She was. These past four days had been different. Better. The station felt lighter with her here, even when she was cataloging violations. She'd stopped being the enemy and become... everything.

"Actually," Lily stood, smoothing her hands down her slacks. "I have news about that."

The bay went quiet. Even the radio seemed to pause its constant chatter.

She walked over, tablet in hand. Professional Lily, but her soft side that wrapped around me last night lived beneath that professional mask.

"I'm finishing my report today." She met my eyes, and something warm passed between us. "The station will receive conditional approval pending minor upgrades. Nothing you can't handle with the current budget allocation."

"Wait." Luke dropped the hose. "You're not shutting us down?"

"No. The violations I found are correctible. With Mason's—Chief Drake's commitment to addressing them within six months, Copper Ridge Fire Department remains operational."

Javi let out a whoop. Luke pumped his fist. I just stood there, staring at her. She'd done it. Found a way to keep us open while still doing her job.

"Thank you," I said, the words inadequate for what I felt.

"I was just doing—"

"No." I stepped closer, not caring who saw. "Thank you."

Her breath caught. For a moment, the rest of the world faded. Just her dark eyes and that almost-smile and the knowledge that we had six more days to figure this out. Six days to convince her that Denver wasn't home anymore. That home was here. With me.

My phone rang.

I pulled it from my pocket without looking away from her. Wyatt's name flashed on the screen. My hands were greasy from checking the engine's fluid levels, so I tapped the speaker button and set the phone on the hood of Engine One. "What do you want, Wyatt?"

"Morning to you too, sunshine." His voice filled the bay, that easy drawl that meant trouble. "That inspector still hanging around?"

Lily went rigid. Shoulders back. Chin up. The Inspector was back in the room.

"Her name is Lily. And yeah, she's here."

"Good. We need to talk about her."

The temperature in the bay dropped ten degrees. Lily's face had gone carefully neutral, but her hands curled into fists at her sides.

"Wyatt—"

"Look, I know you like her. Hell, from what I saw on that video call, you more than like her. But Mason, I did some digging."

"You did what?"

"I was worried, okay? You fall hard and fast, always have. Remember Emily? You were ready to propose after three months and she was already seeing that dentist from Fairplay."

"That's different—"

"Is it? Because from where I'm sitting, you've known this woman a week and you're already gone on her."

Javi shifted uncomfortably. Luke started edging toward the door.

"Wyatt, stop."

But my brother had momentum now, that protective streak that ran in the Drake family like wildfire.

"I found the articles, Mason. Chicago Tribune, Sun-Times..."

"Wyatt, don't."

"Three families sued her, man. Said she froze during a critical evacuation—"

"Shut up." My voice was a low growl.

"—and that her failure to lead directly resulted in the death of Firefighter Derek Lowe. Her fiancé. She resigned in disgrace—"

I grabbed for the phone, but it was too late. I saw the life drain from her face. Her spine went rigid. The woman who'd laughed in my arms last night was gone, replaced by the ghost who'd walked in here eight days ago. She was shutting down. And I couldn't stop it.

"I've got to go." Wyatt's voice softened. "I'm not trying to cause problems, Mason. I just thought you should know who you're getting involved with."

The call ended.

The bay was silent. Javi and Luke were gone. Vanished. Just me and her and the echo of my brother's words hanging in the air like poison.

"Lily—", I started.

She turned away, started gathering her papers with mechanical precision. Her hands shook, scattering documents across the table.

"Lily, I don't care—"

"You don't care?" She spun to face me, and the emptiness in her eyes stole the air from my lungs. "Three families lost someone they loved because I couldn't do my job, and you don't care?"

"That's not what I meant—"

"No, that's exactly what you meant. You think you can fix me. Save me like one of your rescue calls." She laughed, a sharp, ugly sound that had no humor in it. "Poor, damaged Lily. The firefighter who froze. The woman who got her fiancé killed."

"Stop." I reached for her, but she stepped back.

"Is that what this was? Some kind of hero complex? Fix the broken inspector, prove you're better than the guy who died?"

"How can you say that?" Anger flared hot in my chest. "After everything—after this week—"

"It was a mistake."

The words landed like a slap. She gathered the rest of her papers, shoving them into her bag with none of her usual care.

"My report will be filed this afternoon. The station's approved. That's all that matters."

She headed for the door. I followed, catching her arm in the parking lot.

"You're running."

"I'm leaving. There's a difference."

"No, there isn't. Not with you." I moved in front of her, blocking her path to the SUV. "You've been running for two years. From Chicago, from the guilt, from feeling anything. And now you're running from me."

"Get out of my way, Mason."

"No. Not until you listen—"

"To what? More lies about how my past doesn't matter? How those families don't matter?" Her voice cracked. "They sent me letters, did you know that? After Derek died. After their loved ones were injured. They blamed me. And they were right."

"Lily—"

"I stood there, Mason. In the middle of that fire, with my crew looking to me for orders, and I froze. I couldn't move, couldn't think, couldn't breathe. Derek had to take over. Derek died because I failed."

"That's not—"

"Yes, it is!" She shoved past me, keys jangling in her trembling hands. "And you should care about that. You should care that I'm broken. That I'll fail again. That one day I'll freeze when you need me most and you'll die just like Derek did."

"I trust you."

She stopped at her car door, shoulders rigid.

"Did you hear me? I trust you. With my life. With my crew's lives."

"Then you're stupid." She yanked the door open.

"You saved us at the warehouse fire. You didn't freeze then."

"That was different. I wasn't inside. I wasn't—" She cut herself off, jaw tight. "It doesn't matter. None of this matters."

"Eight days ago everything changed. That matters."

"Eight days." She laughed again, that sharp, ugly sound. "Eight days and you think you know me?"

"Lily, please—"

"I'll file my report today. After that, I'm done. With the inspection. With Copper Ridge." She looked at me then, and the finality in her eyes gutted me. "With you."

She started the engine.

"If you leave now, you're proving them right. All those people who said you were a coward."

She pulled out of the parking lot, gravel spinning under her tires. I stood there in the morning sun, watching her drive away, my heart cracked open and bleeding.

Behind me, loud footsteps. Javi appeared at my shoulder.

"Chief—"

"Not now."

"She'll come around. She just needs time to—"

"I said not now."

But even as I walked back into the station, I knew the truth. Time wouldn't fix this. Lily had spent two years building walls around her heart, and I'd torn them down too fast. Now she was rebuilding them, stronger than before.

With me on the outside.

The Running Woman

♥

T he hotel room door slammed harder than I meant it to. My
hands shook as I fumbled with the security latch, sliding it
home. Safe. Locked away. No one could reach me here.

My legs gave out three steps from the door. I hit the scratchy carpet
hard, knees burning through my slacks. The sob that ripped from my
throat sounded animal, raw. Not mine. Couldn't be mine.

But it was.

The tears came in waves, each one dragging me under. My
chest heaved, fighting for air that wouldn't come. The walls pressed
in—wood paneling and faded floral wallpaper closing around me, the
space shrinking to the size of a collapsed room, air growing thin and
hard to find.

Three families sued her.

Wyatt's voice echoed in my skull. Not cruel. Just honest. Just the
truth everyone already knew.

Said she froze during a critical evacuation.

I squeezed my eyes shut. Didn't help. Behind my lids, Derek's face materialized. The Derek from that night. Soot-streaked. Blood trickling from a gash on his temple. His eyes finding mine through the smoke.

Go, Lily. Now.

His last words. An order I'd obeyed while he held that beam. While the building groaned, steel screaming as it twisted above us. While he—

My stomach lurched. I crawled to the bathroom, barely making it before the coffee I'd had at the station came back up. My body shook, rejecting everything. Food. Memory. Mason's touch still lingering on my skin.

Mason.

Fresh tears burned my throat. Eight days. Eight impossible days where I'd let myself believe I could have this. Have him. Have a life that wasn't built on running and regret.

Stupid. So monumentally stupid.

I pushed myself up from the cold tile floor. My reflection in the mirror made me flinch. Mascara tracked down my cheeks in parallel lines. Hair escaping the bun in wild tangles. Eyes red and swollen. This was who I really was. Not the put-together inspector. Not the relaxed woman who'd laughed in Mason's bed. This broken thing that destroyed everything it touched.

Derek was dead because of me.

And Mason. Brave, good Mason, trusting me. He'd followed my directions into that warehouse. What if I'd been wrong? What if the roof had fallen ten seconds sooner? Another name on a list of people I'd failed.

"Stop." My voice cracked in the empty room. "Stop it."

But I couldn't. The spiral had me now, dragging me down into familiar darkness. This was why I'd built the walls. Why I'd wrapped myself in rules and regulations and professional distance. Because the second I let someone in, I put them in danger.

I loved Mason Drake.

The admission knocked the air from my lungs. I loved his rough morning voice and his terrible coffee and the way he commanded a room just by entering it. I loved how he looked at his crew like they were family. How he'd covered me with a blanket that first night. How he'd made me believe, for a few desperate days, that I could be whole again.

And love would get him killed.

I stripped off my clothes—his scent still clinging to my shirt from this morning—and stepped into the shower. The water scalded, but I didn't adjust it. Deserved the burn. Stood there until my skin turned pink and raw, until the hotel's ancient water heater gave up and the spray turned lukewarm.

Clean clothes. Hair back in its bun. Face washed of tears and make-up. Armor rebuilt, piece by piece.

I sat at the small desk and opened my laptop. The cursor blinked in the report field, waiting. I could destroy them if I wanted. List every violation in exhaustive detail. Recommend immediate closure pending full renovation. Make them pay for the pain twisting through my chest.

My fingers hovered over the keys.

Mason in the morning light, making breakfast for his crew. Luke's eager enthusiasm. Javi's steady presence. The town baker pressing that warm pastry into my hand. *Our guardian angel,* she'd called Mason.

I typed:

Copper Ridge Fire Department - Inspection Report

Inspector: L. Zhang

Date: [Today's Date]

Recommendation: CONDITIONAL APPROVAL

The words flowed, professional and measured. Minor violations noted but contextualized. Budget constraints acknowledged. The crew's training and competency highlighted Every word a small goodbye. An apology Mason would never hear.

The station demonstrates strong leadership under Chief Drake and maintains high operational standards despite equipment limitations. With proposed improvements to be completed within six months, CRFD is fully capable of serving the community's emergency response needs.

I stared at the screen. One click would send it. Make it official. End this.

My phone buzzed. Mason. I couldn't answer. But it wasn't a call—it was an email notification.

From: Sarah Lowe

Subject: Please Read This

A cold dread washed through me, so complete it felt like my heart had stopped. Derek's sister-in-law. She'd screamed at me outside the hospital. Called me a murderer while Derek's mother sobbed behind her. Why was she—

Another buzz. Another email. Then another. My inbox flooded with forwards, all from Sarah.

I opened the first with trembling fingers.

Lily,

I know you haven't read my previous emails. I can see they were never opened. That's why I'm sending them all again, and I'll keep sending them until you read them.

We forgive you.

Derek's death wasn't your fault. The investigation proved it—bad intel, structural failure, a dozen factors beyond anyone's control. But more than that, Derek wouldn't want you carrying this guilt. He loved you. He would hate knowing you're punishing yourself for something that wasn't your fault.

The lawsuit was dropped eighteen months ago. Our lawyer pressured us when we were grieving, looking for someone to blame. We were wrong. I was wrong.

Please, Lily. Forgive yourself. Live your life. That's what Derek would want.

Sarah

The words blurred. I scrolled down, opening the forwarded emails. Dozens of them, dating back two years.

Lily, I'm sorry for what I said at the hospital...

We wanted you to know the lawsuit has been withdrawn...

Derek's memorial fund has helped train seventeen new firefighters...

Thinking of you today on the anniversary...

Hope you're finding peace...

Two years of forgiveness I'd been too terrified to see. Too certain of my own guilt to even look.

Another email, from Tom Nowak—one of the injured firefighters:

My lung capacity is at 75% now. Doctors say I might hit 80% by next year. I'm coaching my daughter's soccer team. Life's different but good. Stop blaming yourself for saving most of us. That's what you did, Lily. You saved most of us.

Saved most of us.

The sob caught me by surprise. Different from before—not destruction but release. All this time, I'd been imprisoned by guilt that existed only in my head. They'd forgiven me. They'd moved on. Built new lives from the ashes.

Everyone except me.

My phone rang. Mason's name on the screen. My hand trembled as I reached for it, a wild, impossible hope blooming in my chest. They forgive you. Live your life. Sarah's words. I could answer. I could tell him. We could—

My breath hitched. The hotel room walls tilted. The forgiveness didn't matter. The reports didn't matter. The truth was, I still froze. Even now, just thinking about it, I was back there, paralyzed. It would happen again. With Mason. I would get him killed.

That feeling curdled into pure terror. It was a trap. A cruel trick to make me believe I could be normal, just before I destroyed someone else.

I threw the phone onto the bed as if it were on fire. I had to leave. Not because I didn't love him. But because I did. And loving Mason meant protecting him from me.

I started packing. Mechanical movements—fold, stack, zip. Everything neat and contained, ready to run. My phone buzzed again, but not from Mason.

EMERGENCY ALERT: National Weather Service has issued a RED FLAG WARNING for the following counties... Extreme fire danger due to low humidity and high winds. Outdoor burning banned. Report any signs of smoke immediately.

I moved to the window. The pines outside bent under sudden gusts, and dust devils spun across the parking lot. The sky had taken on that hard, brittle quality that meant no moisture, no mercy. Perfect conditions for disaster.

The fire station sat in the distance, red brick solid against the browning landscape. Mason would be preparing—checking equipment, briefing the crew, watching the horizon. He'd work through the danger because that's who he was. A protector. A guardian angel.

Tomorrow there would be smoke on that horizon. The weather pattern would hold for days, each hour increasing the risk. And when the call came—because it would come—Mason would run toward the flames while everyone else ran away.

Without me beside him.

I pressed my palm against the cool glass. Wished I was brave enough to run toward him instead of away. To choose love over fear. To believe that maybe, possibly, I could be the person he saw when he looked at me.

But I wasn't.

The wind howled, rattling the window in its frame. A storm was coming. I felt it in my bones. I pulled the curtain closed and went back to packing.

Six more days of my inspection window remained, and I'd like to leave now. File the report tonight. I'd have to wait at least two more days before I left according to the guidelines, even if I was just staying in the hotel and catching up .

Alone.

The way it had to be.

The radio in my room—every hotel in fire country had one—crackled to life with updates. Wind speeds increasing. Humidity dropping. Fire weather watch upgraded to warning. Mason's voice cut through briefly, coordinating with dispatch, his tone all business.

My hands stilled on the shirt I was folding. His shirt, I realized. The one I'd stolen that first morning, worn to bed last night. It smelled like smoke and pine and safety.

I sat on the bed, holding it tight. Tonight, I'd let myself remember what it felt like to be loved by Mason Drake. To be seen as someone worth saving.

Even if I couldn't save myself.

The wind picked up another notch, and somewhere in the distance, a siren wailed.

Red Flag Warning

♥

My bags sat by the door, zipped and ready. Outside, the wind howled, sending pine needles skittering across the asphalt of the Mountain View Inn's parking lot. From my second-floor window, I watched storm clouds bruise the peaks. The air had that dry, static-charged feeling, the kind that promised trouble.

Two days. Two days since I'd driven away from the station, from him. Two days of silence that felt louder than any argument. I'd filed my report. The station was approved, with conditions. My job here was done. Tomorrow, I'd be gone. Safe.

A knock on the door made me jump. Three solid raps that echoed in the quiet room.

My pulse thundered.

"Lily." His voice, harsh and low, cut right through the flimsy door. "I know you're in there. We need to talk."

I stood frozen, my hand flying to my throat. I squeezed my eyes shut. Go away. Please, just go away. I crept to the door and looked through the peephole. It was him, haloed by the dim corridor light. He looked like hell—unshaven, exhausted, his broad shoulders slumped.

"Please."

The word was quiet, stripped of his usual command. It cost him something.

I unlatched the security chain. The deadbolt clicked, loud in the silence. I opened the door just six inches, a barrier I desperately needed. His face in the gap was all harsh lines and dark stubble, his eyes searching mine.

"There's nothing to talk about." My voice was flat, professional. The inspector. That's how it had to be.

"Five minutes. That's all I'm asking."

I studied him, my resolve fraying with every second he stood there. The lie was so close. *Go away. I don't want to see you.* But the words wouldn't form.

With a rattling sigh, the chain came free. I opened the door wider.

He stepped inside before I could change my mind, bringing the scent of pine and cold night air with him. The small room seemed to shrink around his presence. His eyes landed on my bags by the door, and all the air seemed to leave his lungs.

"You're leaving," he said. Not a question.

"Tomorrow morning." I moved to the window, needing distance. "My report's filed. Station's approved with conditions. You'll get the official paperwork in a few days."

"I don't give a damn about the paperwork."

I wrapped my arms around my waist, hugging myself. It was an old habit, a useless shield. "You should. It means you can keep your station running."

"Lily—"

"Don't." I turned to face him, lifting my chin. "Whatever you came here to say, it won't change anything. I've made my decision."

"Based on what? My brother being an ass? Because I'm sorry about that. I had no idea he was digging into your past. If I'd known—"

"It's not about Wyatt."

"Then what?" He took a step closer. I backed up until my spine hit the wall. "Tell me what changed. Two days ago you were in my bed. You were laughing. You were—"

"I was being selfish," I cut in, the words sharp. "I was pretending I could have something I can't."

"Why can't you?"

"Because people around me die!" The words ripped from my throat, raw and broken. "Because I freeze when it matters. Because loving me is a death sentence, and I won't do that to you."

The pain in my own voice gutted me. He closed the distance between us in two strides but didn't touch me. Not yet.

"I'm not sorry."

I blinked. "What?"

"I'm sorry my brother hurt you. Sorry he dug up painful memories. But I'm not sorry for falling for you." He let that sink in. "I know it's been ten days. I know that's crazy by any normal standard. I know you think I don't really know you."

"You don't—"

"But I do." He cut me off, his gaze pinning me to the wall. "I know you take your coffee black because cream and sugar feel like indulgences you don't deserve. I know you recheck door locks three times because control makes you feel safe when everything else feels like chaos. I know you twist your hair around your finger when you're thinking hard about something."

My hand dropped from where I'd been doing exactly that.

"I know you haven't laughed—really laughed—like you did last week in two years. Maybe longer." His voice dropped. "I know the scar on your shoulder still aches when it rains. I know you wake up at three a.m. most nights, and that's why you work so late—exhaustion's the only way you can sleep through. I know you're the bravest person I've ever met, even if you can't see it."

Tears tracked down my cheeks. I didn't wipe them away.

"And I know I'm falling in love with you."

The words slammed into me, a force that buckled my knees. I had to lock them to keep from sliding to the floor.

"You can't love me." My voice cracked. "It's been ten days, Mason. Ten days!"

"Tell me you don't feel it too." He moved closer, close enough that I could smell the smoke and pine that always clung to him. "Tell me this is just attraction. Just convenience. Just two lonely people finding comfort." His hand came up, hovering near my cheek but not touching. "Tell me that and I'll walk out that door. You'll never see me again except in passing. I'll respect your choice "

The lie sat right there, ready. *I don't feel it.* Three words and he'd leave. I'd be safe. He'd be safe.

But the words wouldn't come.

"These last two days," his voice broke slightly, "not talking to you, not seeing you, not knowing if you were okay—they've been the longest two days of my life. I think about you constantly. Wake up reaching for you. I can't eat because food tastes like ash without you there to share it."

"Mason—"

"Tell me you don't love me, and I'll go."

The challenge hung between us. All I had to do was lie. Protect him. But I was so tired of lying.

"I can't." The admission was a ragged whisper.

His whole body sagged with relief. 'Lily—"

"But it doesn't matter." I pushed my palms against his chest, a futile attempt to keep him at arm's length. "I love you. God help me, I love you too. But love isn't enough. I don't trust myself. What if I freeze again? What if something happens and I can't—what if I cost you—"

I opened my mouth to list all the reasons this was a mistake, but he didn't let me finish. His mouth was on mine, silencing the spiral before it could drag me under.

The kiss was desperate, consuming, drowning and breathing at the same time. His hands tangled in my hair, holding me like I might disappear. I grabbed his shirt, pulling him closer, needing to crawl inside this moment and live there forever.

We separated, both gasping.

"Don't." His forehead pressed against mine. "Don't spiral. Don't project. Just be here with me."

"I'm scared."

"I know." His thumbs wiped the tears from my cheeks. "But running won't make you less scared. It'll just make you alone."

He kissed me again, softer this time but no less intense. I melted into him, my body overruling every logical objection my brain tried to raise. The kiss deepened, his tongue sliding against mine with a slow, deliberate hunger that made my knees weak.

My fingers trembled as they found the hem of his shirt, dragging it upward, breaking the kiss just long enough to pull it over his head. The sight of him—all hard muscle and golden skin, the tattooed flames wrapping around his arm—made my breath catch. He was beautiful. Mine.

His hands were already working at my sweater, peeling it off with impatient urgency before tossing it aside. The cool air hit my skin, but I barely noticed—his gaze was fire, tracing every inch of me as if he were memorizing me all over again. Then his fingers were at the button of my jeans, popping it open with a rough tug. The sound of the zipper was obscenely loud in the quiet room.

"Lift," he ordered, his voice a low growl, and I obeyed without hesitation, letting him strip the denim down my legs. He knelt before me, his hands gripping my hips as he pressed a kiss to the inside of my thigh, then the other, his breath hot against my skin. Heart rate surged, the sight of him between my legs, aching for more.

His belt buckle clinked as he worked it free, the sound sending a fresh wave of heat through me. Then his jeans were gone, and he was standing before me—naked, hard, perfect. My mouth watered.

I didn't wait for permission. Dropping to my knees, I took him in my hand, stroking him once, twice, before leaning in to press my lips to the head of his cock. His sharp inhale was all the encouragement I needed. I took him deeper, my tongue swirling as I hollowed my cheeks, my free hand cupping his heavy balls.

"Fuck, Lily," he groaned, his fingers tangling in my hair. His grip tensed just enough to guide me, not force me, his thumb brushing my cheekbone as I took him to the back of my throat. "Just like that, baby. So fucking good for me."

I moaned around him, the vibration making his thighs tremble. His praise sent a thrill through me, my own arousal dripping down my thighs. I wanted to please him, to drive him as wild as he made me.

"Look at you," he rasped, his voice like gravel. "Taking me with that pretty little mouth. Such a good girl for me."

His words undid me. I hollowed my cheeks, bobbing my head as I worked him, my hand twisting at the base. His grip on my hair tightened, his hips rocking subtly, feeding me just a little more of him each time.

"Enough," he growled suddenly, pulling me back by my hair. I whimpered at the loss, but then his hands were on me, lifting me onto the bed. He followed, crawling over me, his mouth crashing onto mine as he pushed me back against the mattress.

His fingers found my clit without hesitation, circling with just the right pressure. I gasped into his kiss, my back arching off the bed.

"That's it," he murmured against my lips. "Let me hear you. You're so wet for me, baby. So fucking perfect."

I was already close, my body coiling tight under his touch. But then his fingers slid lower, teasing my entrance before dragging back up to my clit, over and over, never quite giving me what I needed.

"Mason—please," I begged, my nails digging into his shoulders. "I need you inside me."

His chuckle was dark, satisfied. "Since you asked so nicely."

He flipped me onto my stomach in one smooth motion, pulling my hips up until I was on my knees, ass in the air. His hand slid between my legs from behind, two fingers sinking into me with a slow, deliberate thrust.

"Fuck, you're dripping," he groaned. "You want me deep, baby? You want me to fill you up?"

"Yes," I gasped, pushing back against his fingers. "God, yes."

His cock replaced his fingers in one hard thrust, stretching me deliciously. I cried out, my fingers clawing at the sheets as he bottomed out, his hips flush against my ass.

"Like this?" he growled, pulling back before slamming into me again. "You take me so fucking well."

I could only moan in response, the words lost in the overwhelming sensation of him—thick, hard, everywhere. His hand snaked around my hip, finding my clit again, rubbing in tight circles as he fucked me.

"You're mine," he grunted, his pace relentless. "Say it."

"Yours," I sobbed, my orgasm crashing over me like a wave. "Only yours—"

His name tore from my lips as I came, my body clamping down around him. He groaned, his thrusts turning erratic before he buried himself deep with a final, brutal snap of his hips. I felt him pulse inside me, his release spilling hot and thick as he pressed kisses to my shoulder, my spine, my neck.

We collapsed together, a sweaty, trembling mess. He rolled us onto our sides, keeping me pinned against him, his cock still half-hard inside me. His arms wrapped around me, one hand splayed possessively over my stomach, the other tangling in my hair as he pressed his lips to my temple.

"Mine," he said again, softer this time.

"Don't leave," his voice was rough against my neck. "Please don't leave."

Fresh tears burned my eyes. Happy ones this time.

"I filed my report. I could extend my stay, but—"

"Then extend it." He propped himself up on an elbow to look at me. "We'll figure it out. Transfer to the regional office. Consult remotely. Hell, quit and let me take care of you—"

"I'm not quitting my job."

"Then don't. Just... stay. Give us some more time to figure this out."

I traced the tattoo over his heart. "It's crazy. We've known each other for ten days."

"Everything about us is too fast." He captured my hand, brought it to his lips. "Why stop now?"

I laughed. "Move in with me," he said, the words hanging in the air. "I'm serious. Move into the cabin. Wake up with me every morning. Let me make you terrible coffee. Give this a real shot."

He grinned, and the exhaustion fell away, the lines around his eyes crinkling. For a second, he wasn't the chief. He was just a boy, impossibly happy.

"Let me think about it? The moving in part, I mean. I'll extend my stay. Look into the transfer. We can... see how it goes."

"I'll take it." He kissed me, slow and thorough. "I'll take whatever you'll give me."

We talked about logistics—the regional office, my apartment, his terrible internet. It was so normal it felt surreal. Were we really talking about internet providers after I'd just had my soul cracked open and put back together in his arms?

"You should know," I said, tracing patterns on his chest. "I got emails today. From the families in Chicago. They... they forgave me. Dropped the lawsuits eighteen months ago."

His arm wrapped around me. "How do you feel about that?"

"I don't know yet. Relieved? Guilty for feeling relieved? It's... complicated."

"Most things are," he said. "We'll work through it. Together."

Together. The word felt like a coat I was trying on, seeing how it fit.

The wind rattled the windows. Mason's radio, clipped to his jeans on the floor, crackled. We drifted off wound around each other, my fingers linked with his, his heartbeat a steady drum under my ear.

The alarm shattered the pre-dawn quiet.

Not a phone alarm. The fire alarm, blaring from his radio. The one that meant everyone responded.

"All units, all units. Wildfire reported, Devil's Ridge area. Lightning strike. Rapid spread due to wind conditions. Immediate response required."

Mason was already up, pulling on his clothes with practiced efficiency.

"I have to—"

"Go." I sat up, the sheet clutched to my chest. "I'll meet you at the station."

He paused in pulling on his boots. "Lily—"

"I'm not running. Not anymore." I meant it. "Go. They need you."

He bent down and kissed me hard, fast, then was gone.

I reached for my phone. 4:47 a.m. The weather alert showed wind gusts up to 45 miles per hour. Humidity at 12%.

The perfect storm had arrived.

Ten Lives, One Choice

♥

I hit the station floor at a dead run, my boots skidding on the concrete. The apparatus bay was a blur of harsh fluorescent light and moving bodies. My crew. Already pulling on their turnouts. The acrid smell of smoke, sharp and acidic, was already here—an unwelcome guest carried on the wind from Devil's Ridge.

"Talk to me, Javi." I grabbed my coat from the rack, my hands going through the familiar motions on pure muscle memory.

"Lightning strike confirmed at zero-four-thirty. Ridge is fully involved." Javi yanked on his boots, not a wasted motion, his hands finding and securing each buckle in a blur. "Wind's pushing it straight toward town. North-northwest at forty-five miles per hour."

Forty-five. Christ. My teeth ground together as I secured my helmet. At that speed, the fire would vaporize the dry timber.

"Mutual aid?"

"Fairplay's rolling. ETA three hours."

Three hours. I didn't say what we both knew—Copper Ridge would be ash by then.

Luke stumbled through the door, shirt inside out, eyes wide. "Sorry, Chief, I was—"

"Get dressed. Move."

The kid scrambled for his gear. Two more volunteers rushed in—Ed Patterson and his son Mike, both looking grim. Five of us. Five men against what I could already see through the bay doors—a sickening orange pulse against the western sky, as if the sun were setting in the wrong place, burning everything it touched.

"Mount up!"

Engine One roared to life, the diesel engine vibrating through the floorboards. I swung into the passenger seat as Javi took the wheel. Luke and the Pattersons piled into the jump seats. The bay doors were still rising as we rolled out.

The radio crackled. "Dispatch to Engine One. Evacuations ordered for Pine Street, Aspen Court, everything north of Crystal Creek."

I grabbed the mic. "Engine One copies. Any word from the volunteer crews?"

"Negative, Chief. Most are out of town for that training weekend in Denver."

Of course they were. I'd approved the training myself, thinking late spring was safe. Too early for fire season. The weather had other plans.

We crested the hill outside town and the air left my lungs. My stomach didn't just drop; it plummeted. The whole western horizon was on fire. A solid wall of orange, churning smoke into the sky in a column you could probably see from Denver. My mind struggled to process the scale. This wasn't something we could fight. This was something that devoured.

"Madre de Dios." Javi's knuckles went white on the steering wheel.

"We make our stand at the ridge." I pulled up the topographical map on my tablet, though I knew every contour by heart. "Natural firebreak at the creek, then we cut a line along the access road. If it jumps that—"

"It won't." Javi's voice was more hope than certainty.

If it jumps that, the town burns.

We reached the staging area—a wide spot in the dirt road where Forest Service trucks usually parked. Empty now except for one civilian pickup. I recognized it—Jim Harrison, the stubborn bastard who lived in the cabin at the tree line.

"Jim!" I jumped from the engine before it fully stopped. "You need to evacuate. Now."

The old man stood beside his truck, a garden hose in one hand like he planned to defend his property with residential water pressure. "This is my home, Drake. Forty years—"

"And you'll be dead in forty minutes if you don't move." I snatched the hose from him, tossed it aside. "Get in your truck. Drive to town. That's an order."

"You can't order me to—"

The fire crested the ridge behind Jim's cabin with a sound like a freight train. Trees exploded—sap boiling instantly, trunks detonating in the heat. The cabin's roof caught before our eyes, shingles curling like paper.

Jim's protest died in his throat. He dove for his truck, tires spinning gravel as he fled.

I cupped my hands around my mouth, roaring over the noise. "Defensive positions! Javi, get that line deployed. Luke, you're on the pump. Ed, Mike—start clearing brush along the road. Everything within twenty feet gets cut or burned."

We moved like a machine, each of us falling into our roles. Engine One's tank held 500 gallons. At this rate, we had twenty minutes of water. The creek was our only hope for more, but setting up the drafting operation took time we didn't have.

I grabbed the radio. "Dispatch, Engine One. We're establishing defensive line at mile marker twelve. Need water tenders, foam units, whatever you can find."

"Copy, Engine One. Resources are limited. State's mobilizing but—"

"But they'll be too late. I know."

The fire didn't just spread; it hunted, surging down the mountain in waves of flame. Pine trees torched instantly—sixty-foot giants reduced to pillars of fire. The heat hit my face even from a quarter-mile away, dry and fierce enough to crack my lips and sear my lungs.

"Line's ready!" Javi had the hose deployed, a pathetic hundred-foot snake of red rubber against the mountain's rage.

"Hit it!"

Water arced through the air, hissing to steam before it even reached the flames. We might as well have been spitting at the sun.

An hour passed in a blur of smoke and sweat. Then two. My crew rotated positions—man the nozzle until your arms shook, work the pump until your back screamed, cut brush until the chainsaw grew too heavy to lift. The Pattersons tapped out after ninety minutes, exhaustion and smoke inhalation forcing them back.

Three of us now. Three men and one engine against hell itself.

"Chief." Javi's voice was a raw rasp. He coughed, clearing his throat. "We need to pull back."

"No."

"Mason—"

"I said no." I adjusted the nozzle, directing water at a spot fire that had jumped our line. "This is our town. These are our people. We hold."

"We're gonna die holding if—"

The sound of an engine cut through the roar. Not a fire engine—too light. I turned to see a familiar SUV skid to a stop in the gravel. The door opened.

Lily.

She wore borrowed gear—probably from the station's spare closet—the coat too big across her shoulders, the helmet sitting crooked on her head. Her face was pale beneath the brim, but her jaw was set in that stubborn line I now knew meant she wasn't backing down.

"What the hell are you doing here?"

She grabbed a tool bag from the truck bed. "Helping."

"Get back in that truck. Drive back to town. Now."

"No."

"This isn't a discussion, Inspector. You're not cleared for—"

"I'm a trained firefighter." She adjusted the helmet, her fingers certain. "You need more people. I'm here."

"You haven't worked a fire in two years."

"Then it's good I had a refresher this week."

Javi looked between us, reading the situation faster than I'd like. "Chief, we could use—"

"Stay out of this, Martinez."

But Lily was already moving, checking the pressure on a spare tank, testing the weight of a Pulaski. Every movement was muscle memory fighting against rust, competent but careful.

"You don't have to prove anything," I said, my voice quiet, meant only for her.

Her eyes locked with mine through the smoke. "I'm not proving anything. I'm choosing. There's a difference."

Before I could respond, a new engine sound rumbled through the chaos. Three trucks—ranch vehicles with water tanks rigged in the beds. My youngest brother stepped from the lead truck.

James. Cool as a mountain morning in his worn Stetson, as if he drove into wildfires every day.

"Mase." He tipped his hat. "Brought some help. Tom Sullivan, Mike Roper from the Henderson place. Where do you need us?" I nodded, pointing a thumb at Lily, who was already grabbing a fresh tank. "James, this is Lily Zhang. Inspector Zhang, my brother James." They exchanged a quick, smoke-hazed nod—an introduction for another time.

"Javi, get them positioned on the south flank. James, you're running supply—keep those tanks rotating." I turned to Lily. "You're with Martinez. Mop-up only, nothing forward of—"

The radio screamed with static. "All units, emergency traffic! Wind shift, wind shift! Fire is crowning, running east toward residential!"

East. The old neighborhood where the Petersons lived. Where Betty Morrison had refused to evacuate because her cats wouldn't leave. Where the Hendricks family was sheltering with their three kids because they had nowhere else to go.

"How many still in that area?" I called to dispatch.

"Unknown. At least ten, maybe more."

Ten people. Maybe more. The fire would reach them in minutes.

I keyed the command channel. "This is Chief Drake. I need two firefighters for search and rescue, residential sector. High risk."

"That's a one-way trip," Javi said, his voice cropping.

He was right. The fire was crowning—jumping from treetop to treetop, moving faster than a person could run. Anyone going in might not come out.

"I'll go." I started toward my truck. "Javi, you're in command. If mutual aid arrives—"

"Mason, wait—" Lily's voice cut through the chaos.

She stood twenty feet away, her borrowed gear already half-on. For a split second I saw it cross her face—the memory and the fear of Chicago. Her hands trembled on her helmet strap.

Then something shifted. Her jaw set. Her shoulders squared.

"I'll go."

"Like hell you will."

She walked briskly towards me, and when she looked up, I didn't see the haunted inspector anymore. I saw the firefighter she'd been. The one she was choosing to be again.

"You're needed here. Command and control. You know the whole county response—I only know these streets." Her voice was steady, certain. "This is exactly like Chicago. I know that. But this time I'm choosing to go in. Not because I froze and someone had to save me. Because I can save them."

The roar of the approaching fire filled the silence between us.

"Thompson's going with you," I said, my voice rough. "And Tom from the ranch crew. Three-person team minimum."

"Copy that." She finished buckling her gear with practiced efficiency. Every movement was deliberate—not running on instinct, but making a conscious choice with every strap, every check.

Before she turned away, she gripped my arm. "This is me not freezing. Remember that."

"Thompson!" The kid jogged over, eager despite his exhaustion. "You're with Inspector Zhang. Search and rescue, residential sector."

Luke's eyes widened. "Yes, sir."

"Tom, you too." I pointed to one of the ranch hands. "You get in, you get them, you get out. No heroics. No delays."

Lily was already moving, checking her radio, adjusting her gear. I caught her arm as she passed.

"You come back." Not a request. An order. A plea.

"We both know you can't promise that in a fire."

"Say it anyway."

She reached up, her gloved hand resting on my cheek. "I'll come back."

Then she disappeared, Luke and Tom following her into the smoke.

I forced myself to turn away, to focus on the wall of flame that was trying to eat my town. But my radio stayed in my hand, tuned to their channel, waiting.

"Search team, this is Zhang. We're entering the residential area from Oak Street."

Her voice was steady. Professional. The inspector giving a report.

"Copy that." I tried to match her tone. Failed. "Be careful."

James appeared at my shoulder with a fresh water tank. "She'll be okay."

"You don't know that."

"No." He hefted the tank into position. "But I know that look. Saw it in the mirror when I decided to marry Madi despite everyone saying we were too young. Sometimes you just know what you gotta do."

The radio crackled. "Located the Peterson house. Two elderly residents, mobile but slow. Thompson is assisting them to the vehicle."

Relief flooded through me. Two safe.

"Chief, spot fire!" Javi pointed to our left where embers had started a new blaze in the grass. "It's trying to flank us!"

I grabbed a hose line. "James, get a tank over here. Rodriguez, Roper, with me!"

We fought the spot fire while my ears stayed tuned to Lily's frequency. Her voice called out addresses, confirming evacuations, coordinating with Luke and Tom. Each transmission was a small victory, a promise kept.

"Morrison house clear. Hendricks family located—two adults, three children. Loading now."

The main fire roared closer, the heat so intense it felt like standing in an oven. We'd given up ground, pulled back twice, but the town center was still behind us. Still standing.

"That's all of them," Lily's voice came through. "Returning to—wait. There's a car. Someone's trapped."

A cold shock went through my system. "Zhang, withdraw. Now."

"Negative. Driver's unconscious. Door's jammed."

"The fire's right on top of you. Leave it!"

"Thirty seconds."

"Zhang!"

But I could hear it in the background—the sound of metal on metal, Tom's voice shouting, Luke calling out wind direction.

"Got him! We've got him. Moving to evac route—"

Her transmission dissolved into static.

"Lily? Search team, status!"

Silence.

"LILY!"

Ten seconds. Twenty. My world shrank to that dead radio channel. Then: "Search team clear. All residents evacuated. Returning to command."

I folded, bracing my hands on my knees, my lungs fighting for air they seemed to have forgotten how to pull in.

"Chief!" Javi pointed to the horizon. "Look!"

Lights. A line of them, bouncing over the rough road. The Fairplay crew had arrived early, seven engines strong. Behind them, two water tankers from Ridgeway. Even a helicopter materialized from the smoke, its water bucket already full.

"Command, this is Fairplay Chief Rogers. Where do you need us?"

I straightened, pushed the relief down, found my command voice. "Roger, good to hear you. Split your crews. Half on the south flank with my team, half cutting a new break at the ridge. We hold here, we save the town."

The next three hours blurred together. Fresh crews attacking the fire from multiple angles. Water drops from the helicopter. James and his ranch hands running supply like they'd trained for it their whole lives. Slowly, painfully, we started winning.

Dawn was breaking when Lily's team finally returned to command. She emerged from the smoke a ghost of herself—gear torn, face blackened, each movement a study in pain.

She lifted off her helmet, and I ran to her, catching her as her legs buckled.

"Ten people." Her voice was rough, broken. "We got ten people out."

"You got them out. You didn't freeze."

"I was terrified the entire time." She looked up at me, tears carving paths through the grime on her face. "But I did it anyway."

"That's what being brave is."

"Mason, I—" She stopped, coughing, the smoke finally catching up with her.

"Shh. Save it."

"No. I need to say this." She gripped my turnout coat. "I'm done retreating. From fire, from fear, from you. I'm here."

I drew her against me, not thinking about who saw, not caring about anything except the woman in my arms who'd run into hell and come back to me.

"You're here," I whispered into her hair.

"I'm not running anymore." She pressed her face into my neck.

Soot and Sunrise

♥

T he sun crawled over the mountains like it had earned the right to rise. I stood in the apparatus bay, watching golden light spill across concrete still damp from washing down the engines. My borrowed turnout coat hung off my shoulders, three sizes too big, the weight of it pulling at muscles I'd forgotten existed. Every breath tasted like char.

The sounds were muffled, as if coming through cotton. Javi coiled hose, his movements a familiar, steady rhythm in the quiet chaos. On the bumper of Engine One, Luke wasn't crying, but his shoulders shook with the deep, racking tremors of an adrenaline crash I knew all too well. I felt a phantom echo of it in my own limbs. The Pattersons had gone home an hour ago, Ed's arm around his son's shoulders, neither of them speaking.

We'd won. The town stood. Ten people walked out of that inferno because I hadn't frozen.

My legs wanted to buckle.

"Lily!" Rita Brown pushed through the bay doors, arms full of aluminum trays. Behind her, a parade of townspeople streamed in—the baker with boxes stacked to her chin, old Jim Harrison (whose cabin we couldn't save) carrying a coffee urn, Betty Morrison with what looked like every blanket she owned.

"We brought breakfast." Rita set the trays on the folding table someone had dragged out. "Least we could do."

The smell of bacon and eggs turned my stomach. When was the last time I'd eaten? Yesterday? The day before? Time had gone liquid somewhere between the first alarm and now.

"You saved us." Betty grabbed my soot-covered hands, her eyes wet. "You saved my cats, my house, everything."

"The crew—"

"No." Her grip tightened. "You went in. You got us out. Don't you dare minimize that."

A hand landed on my arm, then another on my shoulder. The touches were light, reverent, but they felt like brands. The chorus of "thank you's" became a buzz in my ears, pressing in, stealing the air from my lungs. I wanted to shrink, to disappear. Two years of staying invisible, and now their gratitude was a spotlight I couldn't escape.

"Give the woman some space." Madison Drake's voice cut through the crowd. She moved with the efficiency of someone used to managing chaos, James right behind her carrying what looked like half their ranch kitchen. "Y'all can thank her after she's had food and sleep."

James set down a massive pot of coffee, his movements careful, controlled. Ranch work had given him a different kind of strength than his brothers—quieter, more grounded. He scanned the bay until he found Mason by the equipment racks, checking gear even though we all knew it could wait.

The brothers locked eyes across the space. James tilted his head slightly—a question. Mason's jaw worked, but he nodded once. Whatever conversation they needed was over in three seconds, a lifetime of shared history compressed into gestures I couldn't read.

Madison had already commandeered the serving area, organizing the community offerings with military precision.

"Luke, honey, you need protein." She pressed a plate into the rookie's hands. "Javi, there's fresh salsa from Rosa—she said you'd know what that means."

The crew gravitated toward her warmth like she was the only heat source in a frozen world. She made being taken care of feel like strength instead of weakness.

Mason hadn't moved from the equipment racks. His turnout coat hung open, revealing the department t-shirt underneath soaked with sweat and soot. The morning light caught the exhaustion carved into his face—deeper lines around his eyes, a weight in his shoulders that hadn't been there twelve hours ago.

We hadn't talked. Not about what I'd said at the fire. Not about what he'd said. Not about any of it.

My body made the decision before my brain caught up. I walked to my SUV, each step feeling like swimming through mud. The keys were in the ignition—who locked cars in Copper Ridge? The leather seat accepted my weight, familiar and foreign at the same time.

"Lily."

Mason stood at my window. His hand braced against the door frame, knuckles still raw from some impact I hadn't seen.

"I need to shower. Change." The words came out flat, automatic. "I'll file my report later."

"That's not—" He stopped, ran his free hand through his hair, leaving it standing in ash-gray spikes. "Don't go. Not yet."

The plea in his voice stopped my movement.

"Mason—"

"Just... stay." His eyes met mine, and the commander was gone. This was just a man who'd watched someone he loved walk into fire and nearly not come back. "Please."

I turned off the engine.

He led me through the station, past Madison's organized chaos, past the crew accepting plates and blankets and grateful handshakes. His office door clicked shut, muffling the sounds of recovery.

The couch—that ancient vinyl thing that probably came with the building—had never looked more inviting. Mason sat, and his hand found mine, tugging gently. I folded into him, my head finding the hollow of his shoulder, his arms coming around me like they could shield me from everything we'd just survived.

"Sleep." His voice rumbled through his chest. "Just for a bit."

The last thing I remembered was his lips against my hair and the steady thrum of his heartbeat.

***

I woke to afternoon light and the absence of sound. The station had gone quiet—that deep quiet that meant the crew had finally crashed in their bunks or gone home. Mason's breathing was deep and even beneath me, one arm still wrapped around my waist, the other hanging off the couch.

His face had relaxed in sleep, making him look younger despite the soot still streaking his jaw. A cut I hadn't noticed before ran along his temple, already scabbing over. When had that happened? During the spot fire? When the winds shifted?

His eyes opened, gray as morning fog.

"Hi." The word came out rough, smoke-scraped.

"Hi."

We stayed frozen like that, neither willing to break whatever spell kept us suspended between last night and whatever came next.

"I love you." He shifted so he could see my face better. "I know it's day twelve. I know that's insane by every normal measure. I know you probably think I'm just high on adrenaline or grateful you saved those people or—"

I pressed my fingers to his lips.

"Don't explain it away."

He took hold of my hand, pressed it flat against his chest where his heartbeat kicked into overdrive. Too fast for someone who'd been sleeping.

"Then what the hell am I supposed to do with it? This... feeling. It's like my whole life was in black and white until you walked in. I don't know how to explain it, Lily. I just know it's you."

"I'm broken, Mason." The confession was a raw tear in my throat. "You don't see it, but I... I still wake up choking on smoke that isn't there. My hands..." I looked down at them, flexing my fingers, willing them not to tremble. "Sometimes they just shake. I can't be what you think I am."

"Okay."

"Okay?" I pulled back to see his face. "That's all? Just okay?"

"Did you expect me to run?" His thumb traced the old burn on my shoulder. "Lily, we all have scars. So you wake up at three? I'll be there. Your hands shake? Give them to me." He pressed my hand flat against his chest. "I'm not scared of your ghosts."

His voice caught.

"We're all broken somehow. The difference is whether you face it alone or with someone who gives a damn."

"And you give a damn?"

"I'll be there when you wake up, whatever the time. Every time. I'll check the exits with you. I'll hold you when your hands shake." His forehead pressed against mine. "If you'll let me."

The gravity of that offer—not just love but partnership, not just passion but the daily work of healing—made my chest squeeze.

"I don't know if I can promise—"

"I'm not asking for promises. I'm asking for a chance."

Someone knocked on the door. Three sharp raps that meant business.

"Chief?" Javi appeared in the doorway, not quite looking at either of us. "State's on the phone. They want a preliminary report on the fire response."

Mason's arms cinched around me for just a second before he let go.

"Five minutes."

Footsteps retreated. We sat up, the spell broken, reality creeping back in with all its sharp edges.

"I need time." The words felt like failure, but they were true. "To think. To figure out what I can actually give you."

His face closed off—not angry, just protecting himself from whatever came next.

"How much time?"

"I don't know. A day. Maybe two. I just... I need to not smell like smoke and exhaustion when I make decisions about the rest of my life."

He stood, offered me his hand. I took it, let him pull me up, but he didn't let go.

He took a breath. "The town meeting is in two days. I have to present the budget. Will you be there?"

I couldn't meet his eyes. "My hotel room is booked through Friday."

A muscle worked in his jaw. It wasn't the answer he wanted. It wasn't an answer at all.

"Lily—"

"I should go." I pulled my hand free, already missing the warmth. "You have a phone call."

I made it to the door before he spoke again.

"I meant it. Every word."

I looked back. He stood there in his father's office, covered in soot and exhaustion, offering me everything while I offered him nothing but uncertainty.

"I know."

The door closed between us with a soft click that echoed like a gunshot.

Public Declaration

♥

The Community Center's fluorescent lights hit my eyes like an accusation. Two days. Two days of fighting spot fires across the county, catching three hours of sleep on the station couch, living on stale coffee and protein bars. My shoulders burned from hauling hose, my throat still tasted like ash, and the only thing keeping me upright was knowing this meeting would end soon.

Sixty faces turned toward Mayor Thompson as he shuffled his notes at the makeshift podium. The multipurpose room smelled like the potluck that had preceded the meeting—casseroles and burnt coffee. Folding chairs creaked as people settled in for what promised to be a long discussion about rebuilding.

I scanned the room from my position near the front, where the fire crew always sat during these things. Javi on my right, Luke fidgeting on my left. The Pattersons two rows back. James and Madison against the wall, his arm around her shoulders.

Then I saw her.

Back corner, last row, pressed against the wall like she wanted to disappear into the concrete blocks. Lily. Her hair wasn't in that severe bun anymore—just a loose ponytail that made her look younger, softer. Jeans and a gray sweater instead of her inspector armor. She stared at her hands folded in her lap, avoiding eye contact with everyone.

The knot in my stomach loosened a fraction. She was still here.

Two days of nothing but texts. *I'm okay. Still thinking. Give me time.* I'd typed a dozen responses to each one, deleted them all, sent back: *Take all the time you need.* Even though every hour felt like bleeding out.

"—extensive damage to the western district, but thanks to our fire crew's quick action—"

Thompson's voice droned on. Budget numbers. Insurance claims. Federal disaster relief applications. My eyelids weighed fifty pounds each. The chair felt too small for my frame, my jeans still carrying the ghost-smell of smoke despite two washes.

"Now, the good news." Thompson adjusted his reading glasses. "The state fire marshal's office has completed their inspection of our fire department."

My spine straightened. Across the room, Lily's head came up.

"Inspector Zhang's report came through this week. The Copper Ridge Fire Department has received conditional approval with allocated funding for necessary upgrades." Thompson smiled, that politician's smile that never quite reached his eyes. "We won't be losing our station."

The room erupted. Applause, whistles, someone's "About damn time!" from the back. Javi clapped me on the shoulder hard enough to bruise.

"Furthermore," Thompson raised his voice over the noise, "I want to personally thank Chief Drake and his crew for their heroic efforts during the wildfire. Without them, Copper Ridge would be ash."

More applause. People turned in their seats to look at us. Luke's ears went red. Javi nodded in acknowledgement. I stayed frozen, watching Lily shrink further into her corner.

The mayor kept talking. Statistics about acres saved, structures protected, the valor of our small crew against impossible odds. All true. All incomplete.

My folding chair scraped the floor as I stood. The sound was a gunshot in the quiet room. "There's someone else you should thank." My voice was a gravel-road rasp.

Thompson stopped mid-sentence. Sixty heads turned my way.

I found her eyes across the room. She went rigid. Don't run. Please, Lily, don't run. "Inspector Zhang. Lily Zhang. Stand up."

She shook her head, a tiny, panicked movement.

"During the fire, Inspector Zhang didn't just observe. She coordinated mutual aid. She guided us through the Morrison Building when we had two people trapped and zero visibility. She led a three-person team into an active fire zone and evacuated ten residents who'd refused to leave."

Murmurs rippled through the crowd. Betty Morrison's "That's the girl who saved me!" cut through the noise.

"She did this despite—" My throat closed. Cleared it. Started again. "Despite having left firefighting two years ago after a traumatic incident. She hadn't been inside a working fire since Chicago. But when our people needed help, she went in anyway."

Lily's face had gone pale. Her hands gripped the edges of her folding chair.

"Her recommendations saved our station. Not by going easy on us—she catalogued every violation, documented every deficiency. But she also showed us how to fix them within our budget. She fought for us with the state. She made sure we stayed operational."

The words kept coming, pulled from somewhere deeper than exhaustion.

"She taught me something." My voice dropped, got personal in a way that made my skin crawl. Sixty people leaning forward, but I only saw her. "Rules aren't the enemy. They're not bureaucratic BS designed to make our jobs harder. They exist because someone, somewhere, learned a lesson the hard way. Usually in blood."

Javi shifted beside me. The room held its breath.

"Fear is the enemy. Fear of change. Fear of being wrong. Fear of not being enough." My hands had started shaking. I shoved them in my pockets. "She faced her fears. Walked into that fire despite them. Now I need to face mine."

The fluorescents hummed. Someone's folding chair creaked. In the back corner, Lily had gone completely still.

"Lily Zhang." Her name felt like a prayer and a confession. "I'm terrified of losing you."

A collective intake of breath hissed through the room. Someone behind me muttered, "Holy hell." The sharp crack of ceramic shattering on concrete made me flinch, but I didn't look away from her.

"I'm terrified that two weeks isn't enough. That you'll go back to Denver and forget about this place. About us." My voice cracked. Pushed through. "About me."

She stood. For a second, she just stood there, and my heart hammered against my ribs, certain she was about to turn and walk out the door.

"But I'm more terrified of not trying," I rushed on, desperate. "Of letting you walk away because I'm too proud to beg. Of spending the rest of my life wondering what if."

The room had vanished. Just her, standing there with tears running down her face.

"Stay. Please. Build something with me. With this crew, this town, this life. I know it's crazy. Fourteen days, that's all we've had. But I also know I'll spend the next fourteen years regretting it if I don't ask."

Silence. The kind that presses against your eardrums, makes your heartbeat sound like thunder.

Then she took a step. Then another. She moved between the rows of chairs, a ghost in a gray sweater. Betty Morrison reached out, a silent blessing on her arm. Lily didn't seem to notice. Her eyes were locked on mine. Every step she took was a lifetime. My hands, still shoved in my pockets, were slick with sweat. Was she coming here to say yes, or to tell me I was an idiot in front of my whole town? I wasn't sure I could survive either.

She stopped three feet away. Close enough that I could see the shadows under her eyes, the way her sweater had a small hole near the hem, the slight tremor in her hands.

"You're insane." Her voice barely carried past the front row. "Completely, certifiably insane."

The air punched out of my lungs. It was a no. Of course, it was a no. I'd just humiliated myself, declared my love for a woman I'd known for two weeks in a room full of people I had to lead tomorrow. The fluorescent lights buzzed, suddenly deafening.

"I'm a mess. I have nightmares. Panic attacks. I check door locks obsessively and sleep with three escape routes planned." She took a shaky breath. "This is crazy. No one falls in love in two weeks."

I swallowed hard. "Is that a no?"

She halted before me. Her hand came up to rest against my chest, right over my racing heart.

"That's a yes, you idiot."

I didn't wait for another word. My mouth was on hers. It wasn't a gentle kiss. It was relief. It was desperation. It was a claim. Her arms wrapped around my neck, pulling me down, and she kissed me back with a force that buckled my knees. For the first time in two days, I could breathe.

The room exploded. Whistles, applause, boots stomping on the floor. Someone—probably Luke—let cut a whoop that echoed off the concrete walls. Through the noise, I heard Rita Brown's "Finally!" and Betty Morrison's "I knew it!"

When we looked at each other, Lily's face was flushed, her eyes bright.

She touched my face, thumb tracing my jaw. "We really did this in two weeks."

"Best two weeks of my life."

She laughed, watery but real. "Mine too."

I glanced across the room. James stood against the wall, Madison tucked against his side. He looked at me, tipped his hat in that subtle way that meant everything—pride, approval, brotherhood. Madison wiped her eyes with a tissue, beaming like Christmas had come early.

"Chief Drake?" Mayor Thompson's voice cut through the celebration. He stood at the podium, looking somewhere between amused and exasperated. "If we could perhaps return to the matter of the municipal budget?"

Laughter rippled through the room. I kept my arm around Lily as we walked back to the crew's section. She fit against my side like she'd always belonged there.

"For the record," Thompson adjusted his glasses, fighting a smile, "let the minutes show that Inspector Zhang has agreed to... stay."

More applause. Lily buried her face against my shoulder, but I felt her smile.

The rest of the meeting blurred past. Budget allocations, reconstruction timelines, federal grant applications. Important stuff that I'd review later when my brain worked again. Right now, all that mattered was Lily's hand in mine, her thumb tracing circles on my palm, the quiet promise of it.

When Thompson finally adjourned the meeting, people swarmed us. Betty Morrison hugged Lily so hard she squeaked. The Pattersons shook my hand until my arm went numb. Javi muttered something about "took you long enough" before pulling us both into a crushing embrace.

Through it all, Lily stayed pressed against my side. My anchor in the chaos.

"You really did that." Her voice was soft, meant just for me despite the crowd. "Stood up in front of everyone."

"You walked into a burning building for this town. Least I could do was admit I love you in front of it."

She went up on her toes, pressed her lips to my ear.

"I love you too. In case that wasn't clear."

Sullivan Ranch

♥

Four weeks since I'd driven into Copper Ridge with my clipboard and my armor and my certainty that rules would keep me safe. Now Mason's truck wound up the dirt road to Sullivan Ranch, and I barely recognized myself in the passenger seat. Hair loose around my shoulders. His hand resting on my thigh. The diamond on my finger catching afternoon light—small, simple, perfect. He'd proposed yesterday morning over terrible station coffee, down on one knee in the apparatus bay while Javi pretended not to film it on his phone.

"Stop counting." Mason's thumb traced circles on my knee.

"Can't help it. My brain keeps doing the math. We met four weeks ago. Got engaged yesterday. My mother would have a full-blown, clutching-her-pearls aneurysm."

"Your mother will love me." He turned onto the ranch property, cattle gates open. "Does she know you saved me from a burning building? I need you."

The ranch house sat against the mountain backdrop like it had grown from the earth itself. Log construction, wraparound porch, flower boxes Madison tended with religious devotion. Smoke curled from the chimney despite the afternoon warmth. Through the kitchen window, I caught movement—Madison at the stove, James setting the table.

"They didn't have to do this." The knot in my stomach constricted. "Dinner, the celebration—"

"They're family." Mason killed the engine. "This is what family does."

Family. The word lodged in my throat. Two years of isolation, of keeping everyone at arm's length, and now I had a whole town claiming me. Soon to be brothers-in-law..

The front door opened before we reached the porch. Madison Drake stood in the doorway, the afternoon sun backlighting her so she was just a silhouette with flour on her apron, her smile genuine.

"There you are!" She pulled me into a hug that smelled like vanilla and bread. "James has been checking the window every five minutes."

"Have not." James appeared behind his wife, hat in hand. The youngest Drake brother moved with the unhurried confidence of someone who'd found his place early and never questioned it. "Maybe every ten minutes."

Mason's hand found the small of my back as we entered. The house wrapped around us—warm wood, family photos spanning generations, the comfortable chaos of a life fully lived. A dog—some kind of retriever mix—thumped its tail from a bed near the fireplace. The kitchen overflowed with food: roast beef, mashed potatoes, green beans from Madison's garden, rolls still steaming from the oven.

"This is too much—"

"This is dinner." Madison steered me to a chair. "Sit. Mason, get her some wine. The good stuff James pretends he's not hiding in the pantry."

"That's for special occasions," James protested.

Madison's hand brushed her husband's arm. "Your brother getting married isn't special enough?"

James passed his wife, his hand finding her waist in a move so automatic he didn't even notice. She leaned into the touch for a split second, a silent communion that started an ache behind my ribs. It was quickly replaced by the solid warmth of Mason's hand, still resting on my back.

Dinner unfolded in laughter and stories. James regaling us with tales of teenage Mason trying to father him and Wyatt. Madison adding color commentary about the time she'd caught all three Drake boys skinny-dipping in the creek. Mason's ears turned red, but he laughed, his hand finding mine under the table.

"Speech time." James stood, raising his beer. The dining room light caught the gray starting at his temples, premature from sun and wind. "I was eleven when Dad died. Mason was sixteen. Could've let the family fall apart. Instead, he held us together. Raised us, really."

Mason shifted beside me, uncomfortable with praise.

"Never thought I'd see him let someone take care of him." James's eyes found mine. "But here we are. To Mase, who finally pulled his head out of his ass." Mason scoffed. "And to Lily," James continued, his eyes softening. "For showing him what he was missing. Welcome to the family. Lord knows you're brave enough for it."

The words hit harder than expected. Brave enough for it. Not brave enough to run into fire—I'd done that. But brave enough to stop running. To choose roots over rules.

"Welcome to the family, Lily." Madison's eyes sparkled with tears she blinked away. "Fair warning—Drake men love hard and forever. Hope you're ready."

"Nobody's ever ready for a Drake man." I found my voice, surprising myself. "You just hang on and hope for the best."

James barked a laugh. "She's got your number, Mase."

After dinner, Madison insisted on showing me the guest cabin. "James remodeled it. We rent it out, but tonight it's yours." She squeezed my hand at the door. "Take all the time you need. We'll handle the cleanup."

The cabin sat fifty yards from the main house, tucked into a grove of aspens. Small but perfect—one room with a stone fireplace, queen bed piled with quilts, windows facing the mountains. James had already lit a fire, and the space glowed with warmth.

Mason closed the door, and the silence of the cabin pressed in. The numbers started ticking in my head like a bomb. Twenty-eight days. Four weeks. Engaged. A cold wave washed through me, and I had to grip the windowsill to stay upright.

"You're doing it again," he said, crossing to where I stood. "The counting thing."

"How are you not freaking out?" I turned to face him. "This timeline is insane. We're insane."

"Probably." He reached up, tucked hair behind my ear. "But I'd rather be crazy with you than sane without you."

"My therapist would have a field day with this."

"What would she say?"

I considered. "That I'm replacing one form of running with another. That I'm using you to avoid dealing with my trauma. That crash relationships after loss are rarely healthy."

"Does she know how you feel in my arms? Tell her that."

"She'd probably say that's more evidence." I stepped into him, my hands finding his chest. "And I don't care."

"Do you regret it?"

The question hung between us. Did I regret the desperate kiss in his office? The night in his cabin when we'd torn into each other like drowning people finding air? The choice to stay when every instinct screamed run?

"Not even a little bit."

His mouth found mine, different from every kiss before. Not desperate. Not claiming. Just... certain. Like we had all the time in the world because we'd already decided on forever.

"Bed." The word rumbled against my mouth.

"It's seven-thirty."

"And?"

He walked me backward until my knees hit the mattress. The fire crackled, painting shadows on the walls. Through the windows, the last sunlight faded behind the peaks. This far from town, the silence was complete. Just us and the mountains and the promise of what came next.

His hands found the hem of my sweater, paused.

"We can just sleep. Talk. Whatever you need."

"I need you." I pulled the sweater over my head. "I need this."

He made a sound low in his throat, fingers tracing the fabric of my bra. "Still so beautiful."

"Even the scar?"

His eyes found the puckered skin on my shoulder—the place where Chicago had marked me forever. He lowered his head, pressed his lips to the worst of it. He traced the edge with a single finger, reverently, then looked up at me. "All of it, Lily. Every part of you. It's all mine now."

My throat closed. "Mason—"

"Every single thing that happened to you, every choice, every moment of pain—it all led here. To us. I wouldn't change any of it."

He lowered me to the bed with infinite care. No desperation now, no race against time. We'd already won that battle. This was just... us.

Mason and Lily. Building something from the ashes of what we'd been before.

"I want to tell you something." He settled beside me, his hand tracing patterns on my stomach. "All the ways I plan to love you."

"All of them?"

"Every single one." His mouth found my neck, speaking against skin. "Going to wake up with you every morning. Make you terrible coffee. Better than hotel coffee but still pretty bad."

I laughed, the sound escaping without thought.

"Going to fight with you about regulations." His teeth scraped my collarbone. "You'll be right half the time. Maybe more. Don't tell anyone I said that."

"Your secret's safe."

"Going to hold you when the nightmares come." His voice dropped, serious now. "Every time. Middle of the night, middle of the day, doesn't matter. You won't be alone with them anymore."

The tears came without warning. 'I still have them. The nightmares. Less now, but—"

"I know." He pulled me against him, my back to his chest, arms wrapped around me like armor. "Heard you last night. Four a.m. You went to the kitchen, made tea, sat at the table until dawn."

"You were awake?"

"Always am when you are." His lips found my ear. "Just giving you space to process. But after we're married? No more space. You wake up scared, you wake me up too. Deal?"

"Deal."

His hand slid lower, teasing. "What else? Going to make you breakfast every morning. Pancakes on Sundays. Going to teach you to ride—James has horses."

"I know how to ride."

"Motorcycles?"

"Mason Drake, you do not own a motorcycle."

"Not yet." He grinned against my shoulder. "But Wyatt's selling his. Figured we could use some excitement."

"Because our life has been so boring so far."

"Going to love you through every season," he growled, his voice soothing me, "Summer fires. Winter storms. Whatever comes."

I swallowed hard, my pulse hammering between my thighs. "That's a lot of promises."

His mouth curved—predatory, possessive. "Just getting started."

Then his lips crashed down on mine, hot and demanding, his tongue sweeping in to claim me. I gasped into the kiss, my fingers digging into the hard planes of his shoulders as he devoured me. He didn't just kiss—he conquered, his teeth nipping my lower lip before soothing the sting with a slow, wet stroke of his tongue.

When he finally pulled back, his breath was ragged, his gaze locked on me like I was the only thing in the world. "Mine," he murmured, more vow than word, before his mouth trailed down my throat.

I arched into him as he kissed, licked, bit—each press of his lips sending a jolt straight to my core. His calloused hands slid down my sides, rough against my skin, before his fingers traced the sensitive undersides of my breasts. A whimper tore from my throat when he finally, finally palmed them, his thumbs brushing over my nipples until they ached.

"Mason—"

"Shh." His voice was a dark purr against my collarbone. "Let me taste you."

Before I could protest—before I could even breathe—he was gone, his broad shoulders wedging between my thighs as he dragged me to the side of the bed. The first swipe of his tongue was a shock, hot and wet and relentless, and I cried out, my back bowing off the mattress.

"Oh god—"

His hands gripped my hips, holding me still as he feasted, his tongue delving between my folds before circling my clit with slow, deliberate strokes. Every lick was a brand, every suck a claim. He groaned against me, the vibration making my thighs tremble, and when he slid two thick fingers inside me, curling them just right, I shattered with a broken scream.

He didn't stop.

He lapped at me through the aftershocks, his free hand sliding up to pinch my nipple, drawing out every last shudder. Only when I was boneless and gasping did he finally lift his head, his lips glistening, his eyes dark with hunger.

By the time he crawled back up my body, I was a trembling mess, my skin oversensitive, my breath coming in ragged gasps. He loomed over me, his cock thick and heavy against my thigh, the tip already wet.

"Look at me," he ordered, his voice a dark rasp.

I forced my eyes open, meeting his gaze. The raw, possessive love in his expression stole my breath.

"Mine," he said again, not a question, not a request—a fact.

"Yours," I whispered.

A growl tore from his chest as he flipped me onto my hands and knees, his hands gripping my hips as he dragged me back against him. The head of his cock teased my entrance, and I moaned, pushing back, desperate.

"Not like this," he grunted, his voice uneven. "I want to see you."

Before I could process the words, he was pulling me up, his hands wrapping around my wrists, guiding them behind my back. His fingers laced with mine, holding me captive as he settled onto the bed, his powerful thighs spread, his cock jutting up between us.

"Ride me," he commanded, his grip unyielding. "Just like that. Hands behind your back. Let me watch you take what's yours."

I hesitated for only a second before straddling him, my knees sinking into the mattress on either side of his hips. The moment I sank down, we both groaned—him thick and full inside me, stretching me perfectly, me clenching around him, my body already greedy for more.

"Fuck, Lily," he hissed, his hips jerking up as I started to move. "Just like that. Take me deep."

His hands easing around mine, keeping me trapped as I rode him, my breasts bouncing with each roll of my hips. The angle was perfect, his cock hitting that spot inside me that made my toes curl, my breath hitch.

"Mason—I can't—"

"You can," he growled, his thighs flexing beneath me, driving up into me harder. "You're taking me so fucking well. Look at you. Love that tight pussy."

The word sent a fresh wave of heat through me, my walls fluttering around him. His grip on my hands was bruising, his control slipping as I tightened around him, my movements growing erratic.

"Come for me," he demanded, his voice a dark snarl. "Now, Lily. Now."

The command sent me over the edge, my back arching as pleasure crashed over me, my cry ringing through the room. Mason followed with a guttural groan, his cock pulsing inside me as he spilled deep, his body locking up beneath mine.

For a long moment, neither of us moved, our ragged breaths the only sound in the room. Then, slowly, he released my hands, his fingers trailing up my arms before pulling me down against his chest.

We collapsed like that, tangled in each other, the fire burning low. His heart hammered beneath my ear, his skin slick with sweat. I felt him everywhere—inside me, around me, owning me.

And for the first time in years, I wasn't afraid.

I was his.

"So." I pressed a kiss to the tattoo over his heart. "Wedding timeline."

"Tomorrow?"

"The courthouse is closed on Sundays."

"Monday then."

I laughed. "Your mother would murder you. She's already called twice about venues."

"Six months?" He grasped my hand, kissed my ring finger just above the diamond. "Give people time to stop gossiping, plan something proper?"

"Six months." I agreed. "Though someone will definitely think I'm pregnant."

"Are you?"

"No." I swatted his chest. "But Ruby at the salon is already speculating. Javi told me."

"Of course she is." He pulled me closer. "Speaking of the future—you decide about the job?"

"I accepted yesterday. Regional fire safety coordinator. I can work from here, travel when needed."

"Based in Copper Ridge?"

"Based wherever you are."

He went still. "Lily—"

"I know what I'm choosing. Small town. Smaller job. Life with a firefighter who runs toward danger."

"That what you want?"

"What I want is you. Morning coffee, even if it's terrible. Fighting about regulations. Pancakes on Sundays." I found his eyes in the dying firelight. "The nightmares will come. I'll have bad days. Might freeze again sometime when it matters."

"Then we'll work through it."

"That simple?"

"That simple."

His phone buzzed on the nightstand. He ignored it. It buzzed again.

"Could be the station—"

"I'm off duty." But he reached for it anyway, years of conditioning. "It's Wyatt."

The screen lit his face as he read. A grin spread slowly.

"What?"

"Says he'll be at the wedding. Wouldn't miss his big brother making an honest woman out of the inspector."

"That's sweet—"

"Also wants to know if your friend Emma still needs a summer rental. Says his buddy has a cabin available."

I sat up. "Emma? From Denver? How does he know about Emma?"

"I might have mentioned you had a writer friend looking for a quiet place to finish her book." Mason's grin turned wicked. "Might have mentioned she was single. And gorgeous."

"You've never met Emma."

"Saw her Instagram. You tagged her last month."

"Mason Drake, are you matchmaking?"

"Just passing along information." He pulled me back down. "Though if my brother happened to be in town when she arrives..."

"He runs. You said he never stays anywhere longer than a season."

"Things change." His arms stretched around me. "People surprise you. Look at us."

"Twenty-eight days."

"Best twenty-eight days of my life."

"So far."

"So far," he agreed, and kissed me again as his phone lit up with another text from Wyatt.

Lightning Strikes Twice

♥

People say you can't fall in love in ten days.

They're wrong.

You can. But you spend the next ninety proving it to yourself.

I smoothed the blue fabric of my dress—still strange not wearing a suit—and caught my reflection in the station's glass doors. Three months since I'd first walked through these same doors with my clipboard and my certainty that rules would keep the world safe.

"You ready for this?" Mason's hand found my lower back, warm through the thin fabric.

"For our engagement party or for whatever's about to happen with your brother?"

His lips quirked. "Both?"

Through the open bay doors, checkered cloths and string lights had transformed the apparatus floor. The engines sat outside in the lot, their usual spots taken by rented tables covered in checkered cloth. String lights crisscrossed overhead, and the smell of Rita's famous chili competed with Betty Morrison's apple pie. Half the town had already arrived, filling the space with conversation and laughter.

"Lily!" Luke Thompson bounded over, his girlfriend Sarah trailing behind. "The decorations look amazing. Did you—"

"That was all Madison." I nodded toward the corner where James's wife directed the placement of another casserole dish. "She's got a gift for this stuff."

Luke's expression shifted to concern. "Is it true Wyatt's coming tonight?"

Mason's hand tensed against my back. "He said he would."

"Cool. Cool." Luke bounced on his heels. "And that writer friend of yours, Lily? Emma?"

The question hung between us. Mason and I had been dancing around this topic for weeks—Emma arriving tomorrow for her summer rental, Wyatt deciding to stick around Copper Ridge instead of heading to Montana for fire season. The timing wasn't a coincidence; it was a planned collision.

"She'll be here." I kept my voice neutral. "Driving up from Denver."

Sarah tugged Luke toward the food table before he could ask more questions, leaving Mason and me standing at the threshold of our own party.

"Six months." He turned me to face him, fingers tracing the edge of my jaw. "Think people will stop talking by then?"

"About us getting married six months after we met?" I leaned into his touch. "Never. But Ruby at the salon is already taking bets on whether I'll be showing by the ceremony."

"Are you?"

"Still no." I swatted his chest, but I was smiling. "Though at this rate, half the town will be disappointed."

"They'll live." He kissed me, quick but thorough, before leading me into the celebration.

The next hour passed in a blur of congratulations and well-wishes. Javi made a toast that had everyone laughing and me hiding my face against Mason's shoulder. The band played bluegrass versions of love songs, and couples swayed on the makeshift dance floor.

I was refilling my punch glass when Madison appeared at my elbow, practically glowing.

"Don't drink too much of that." She gestured at the punch bowl. "Rita spiked it with something that could strip paint."

"Speaking of not drinking..." My gaze dropped to where her hand rested on her stomach, the slightest curve visible under her flowing dress.

Her smile bloomed. "Twelve weeks. We wanted to wait until we were sure."

"Madison!" I pulled her into a careful hug. "That's amazing. James must be over the moon."

"He's already picked out names. Built a crib. The man's been ready to be a father since the day we got married." Her eyes glistened. "It just took longer than we planned."

James materialized beside his wife, his hand finding that spot on her lower back that Mason favored with me. The youngest Drake brother had dressed up—pearl snap shirt, his best jeans, boots that had seen polish.

"Everything okay?" His voice carried that gentle concern that defined him.

"Just telling Lily our news." Madison leaned into him, and his whole face softened.

"About time we added to the Drake family chaos." James's gaze found Mason across the room. "Mase know yet?"

"Go tell him." I squeezed James's arm. "He'll want to hear it from you."

James made his way through the crowd toward his brother. Mason was mid-conversation with the mayor, but he turned immediately when James approached. He didn't say a word, just tilted his head. Mason raised an eyebrow. James made a small gesture—a hand curving in the air—and a slow grin spread across Mason's face. He knew.

Mason grabbed his brother, pulled him into one of those half-hug, back-slapping embraces that Drake men specialized in. They separated quickly, but Mason's hand stayed on James's shoulder, squeezing once. James said something that made Mason's throat work. A pause. Then James nodded toward the mountains visible through the bay doors, and I knew without hearing that he'd mentioned their father.

The front door banged open.

Wyatt Drake stood backlit in the entrance, wearing dark jeans and a henley that had seen better days. His hair was longer than in the photos Mason kept, sun-bleached and wind-tossed. He carried himself differently than three months ago—less perpetual motion, more deliberate presence.

"Sorry I'm late." He scanned the crowd until he found Mason. "Got held up in—"

Another car door slammed outside.

Emma Reed appeared in the doorway, looking for all the world like someone who'd driven six hours and walked into the wrong party. Her petite frame was drowning in an oversized sweater, dark hair pulled into a messy bun, uncertainty written across her features.

"Lily, I know I'm early, but I thought—"

Her words died as her gaze landed on Wyatt.

The chatter in the station collapsed into a sudden, ringing silence. The band's bluegrass tune faltered, a fiddle note dying in the dead air.

"You."

They said it simultaneously, twin expressions of recognition and shock rippling across their faces.

Emma's face drained of color. Wyatt's jaw went rigid. The air between them went tight, heavy. Wyatt's easy posture vanished, his shoulders locking into a rigid line. Emma flinched as if he'd shouted, though he hadn't said a word.

"You two know each other?" Mason had moved beside me, his voice low and even, betraying nothing.

Wyatt's laugh was sharp, bitter. "You could say that."

Emma's hands gripping her car keys. "It was a long time ago."

"Five years." Wyatt's voice dropped, each word precise.

"Wyatt—"

"You left." He took a step toward her. "No note. No explanation. No goodbye. Just gone."

The crowd had formed a subtle circle, pretending not to watch while absolutely watching. Ruby from the salon was already on her phone, probably texting everyone who wasn't here.

Emma's chin lifted, a flash of the steel that I knew lived beneath her gentle exterior. "You were leaving anyway. For Alaska. Remember? Another fire season, another state, another—"

"Another excuse for you to run?"

The words landed like a slap. Emma took a step back, bumping into the door frame.

"I should go." She turned, but I moved faster, catching her arm.

"You just drove six hours." I kept my voice low, steady. "At least have some food first."

Her eyes were bright with unshed tears. "Lily, I can't—"

"Yes, you can." Madison appeared on Emma's other side, all maternal warmth despite barely knowing her. "I'm Madison, James's wife. You must be exhausted. Let's get you a plate."

Together we guided Emma toward the food table, leaving the brothers standing in our wake. I glanced back to see James murmuring something to Wyatt, Mason's hand on Wyatt's shoulder.

"Five years?" Madison's question was gentle as she handed Emma a plate.

"We met at a writing conference in Portland." Emma's voice was barely audible. "I was there for a workshop. He was fighting fires in Oregon, had the weekend off. We..."

"Had one perfect night?" I asked softly.

Emma's laugh was watery. "Three perfect days, actually. And then I looked up his crew schedule. Saw he'd be gone nine months out of twelve. Different states, different fires, never stopping. I couldn't—" She stopped, started again. "My dad was military. Gone more than he was home. I swore I'd never..."

"Never fall for someone who leaves." Madison's voice carried understanding.

Emma nodded, miserable.

Across the room, Wyatt had grabbed a beer, his knuckles white around the bottle. Mason said something that made him shake his head sharply. James added something else, and Wyatt's shoulders dropped a fraction.

"Want to know something funny?" Emma watched him through the crowd. "I've compared every man since to those three days. None of them measured up."

The band started playing again, the fiddle player launching into something upbeat that got people moving back to their own conversations. The immediate drama had passed, but the tension remained, threading through the party like smoke.

An hour later, I found myself on the makeshift dance floor with Mason, swaying to something slow and sweet. Wyatt stood by the bay doors, nursing his third beer, tracking Emma's every movement. She'd relaxed enough to chat with Dr. Sarah, but her gaze kept drifting to him.

"Think lightning can strike twice?" Mason murmured against my ear.

"In this town? Definitely."

James's voice carried from behind us, dry as summer kindling. "Lightning's got nothing on Drake men. We don't strike twice—we strike once and stick."

Madison laughed, elbowing him gently. "Smooth, cowboy."

He grinned, pressed his lips to her temple, his hand spreading protectively over where their child grew.

The four of us stood together, watching the delicate dance of Wyatt and Emma not talking to each other. They'd orbited all evening—never closer than ten feet, never farther than line of sight. The pull between them was a tangible thing; every time she moved, his head turned, his body angled toward her like a compass finding north.

"He's going to stay because of our wedding." Mason's voice carried quiet certainty. "First time in fourteen years he's turned down a fire season."

"She's rented the cabin for three months." I leaned into his warmth. "That's a long time to avoid someone in a town this small."

"Or a long time to figure things out." Madison's smile was knowing.

The party wound down slowly, people drifting away with promises to see us at the wedding. Emma slipped out during a wave of departures, but not before I saw Wyatt's head turn to track her exit.

Mason and I stayed to help clean up, stacking chairs and pulling down lights while the crew swept the floor. The station settled back into itself—engines returned to their bays, gear hung in its proper place, the eternal smell of coffee already brewing for the night shift.

"Hey." Mason caught me as I carried the last box of decorations to the storage closet. "You good?"

I set the box down, wrapped my arms around his waist. "I spent five years running from fire. Turns out, I just needed to find the right one to run toward."

His hands framed my face. "Fast or slow, doesn't matter. Real is real."

"Real is real." I pulled him down for a kiss that tasted like promises and forever and home.

Behind us, the station settled into its nighttime rhythm—radio chatter, the tick of cooling engines, someone starting dinner prep in the kitchen. Through the windows, Copper Ridge spread out under stars, porch lights glowing like earthbound constellations.

This place had become home. These people had become family. And Mason—Mason had become everything.

The future stretched ahead, bright with possibility. A wedding in three months. A new Drake baby. Whatever was going to happen between Wyatt and Emma.

Real was real.

And this? This was as real as it got.

Embers To Inferno

Get the first book in the series, the story of James and Madison Drake for free!

Go To: books.vabrowning.com/wildfire-hearts-prequel

About the author

♥

V .A. Browning writes contemporary romance that sizzles with workplace tension and authentic emotional depth. Her passion for storytelling was born from years of being a voracious reader who devoured romance novels by the stack, always searching for stories that balanced smart, capable characters with the messy, wonderful reality of falling in love. After spending over a decade in the hospitality industry, she discovered that the high-pressure, fast-paced world of hotels and restaurants provided the perfect backdrop for the kind of intense, slow-burn romance she loves to read—and write.

Her novels draw directly from her professional experience, bringing insider knowledge to stories about driven characters who find love in the most unexpected places. V.A. specializes in workplace romance featuring competent, passionate people who are masters of their professional domains but complete disasters when it comes to matters of the heart. She believes the best love stories happen when two people let their carefully constructed armor crack just enough to let someone else in, and she's particularly drawn to exploring how cultural heritage and family legacy shape the way we love.

When she's not crafting the perfect enemies-to-lovers dynamic or perfecting a hero's swoon-worthy declaration scene, V.A. can be found in her cozy home office overlooking her garden, usually with a diet coke within arm's reach and her two rescue dogs—a mischievous Whippet named Louie and a silly Boxer named Rocky—sprawled at her feet. Her ideal Sunday involves farmers market visits for fresh flowers and artisanal coffee, followed by afternoon sewing sessions where she creates quilts from vintage fabrics she's collected over the years. She's a firm believer that the best stories, like the best meals, are meant to be savored slowly.

V.A. is passionate about representing authentic cultural experiences in her work. She lives in Oklahoma with her two dogs, an ever-growing collection of fabric scraps, and enough romance novels to stock a small bookstore. She's currently working on her next novel, another workplace romance that promises to deliver the same blend of professional competence, cultural richness, and irresistible romantic tension that readers expect from her stories. When readers ask her about her writing philosophy, she always says the same thing: every reader deserves a happily-ever-after that feels both swoon-worthy and real, featuring characters who are passionate, flawed, and deeply, beautifully human.

Learn about all the books she has available at www.books.vabrowning.com